Meg Cabot is the author of many books for young adults, including the phenomenally successful *The Princess Diaries* series, *All American Girl*, *Nicola and the Viscount* and *Victoria and the Rogue*, as well as several books for adult readers. With her husband and one-eyed cat, Henrietta, she divides her time between Florida and New York City, and says she is still waiting for her real parents, the king and queen, to restore her to her rightful throne.

Visit Meg Cabot's website at w

Also by Meg Cabot

The Mediator 1: Love You to Death

The Princess Diaries
The Princess Diaries: Take Two
The Princess Diaries: Third Time Lucky
The Princess Diaries: Mia Goes Fourth
The Princess Diaries: Give Me Five
The Princess Diaries: Sixsational

The Princess Diaries Guide to Life
The Princess Diaries Princess Files

The Princess Diaries: Mia's Christmas

All American Girl

Nicola and the Viscount
Victoria and the Rogue

Look out for
The Mediator 3: Mean Spirits

Teen Idol

And for adults

The Guy Next Door
Boy Meets Girl

THE MEDIATOR 2
High Stakes

Meg Cabot

MACMILLAN CHILDREN'S BOOKS

First published 2001 as *Ninth Key* under author name Jenny Carroll by Pocket Pulse
an imprint of Simon and Schuster, USA

This edition published 2004 by Macmillan Children's Books
a division of Macmillan Publishers Limited
20 New Wharf Road, London N1 9RR
Basingstoke and Oxford
www.panmacmillan.com

Associated companies throughout the world

ISBN 0 330 43738 0

1 3 5 7 9 8 6 4 2

A CIP catalogue record for this book is available from the British Library.

Typeset by Intype Libra Ltd
Printed and bound in Great Britain by Mackays of Chatham plc, Kent

To Vic and Jack —
Cut it out already

One

Nobody told me about the poison oak.

Oh, they told me about the palm trees. Yeah, they told me plenty about the palm trees, all right. But nobody ever said a word about this poison oak business.

'The thing is, Susannah—'

Father Dominic was talking to me. I was trying to pay attention, but let me tell you something: poison oak *itches*.

'As mediators – which is what we are, you and I, Susannah – we have a responsibility. We have a responsibility to give aid and solace to those unfortunate souls who are suffering in the void between the living and the dead.'

I mean, yeah, the palm trees are nice and everything. It had been cool to step off the plane and see those palm trees everywhere, especially since I'd heard how cold it can get at night in northern California.

But what is the deal with this poison oak? How come nobody ever warned me about *that*?

'You see, as mediators, Susannah, it is our duty to help lost souls get to where they are supposed to be going. We are their guides, as it were. Their spiritual liaisons between this world and the next.' Father Dominic fingered an unopened pack of cigarettes that was sitting on his desk, and regarded me with those big old baby blues of his. 'But when one's spiritual liaison takes one's head and slams it into a locker door . . . well, you can see how that kind of behaviour might not build the sort of trust we'd like to establish with our troubled brothers and sisters.'

I looked up from the rash on my hands. Rash. That wasn't even the word for it. It was like a fungus. Worse than a fungus, even. It was a *growth*. An insidious growth that, given time, would consume every inch of my once smooth, unblemished skin, covering it with red, scaly bumps. That oozed, by the way.

'Yeah,' I said, 'but if our troubled brothers and sisters are giving us a hard time, I don't see why it's such a crime if I just haul off and slug them in the—'

'But don't you see, Susannah?' Father Dominic clenched the pack of cigarettes. I'd only known him a couple of weeks, but whenever he started fondling his cigarettes – which he never, by the way, actually smoked – it meant he was upset about something.

That something, at this particular moment, appeared to be me.

'That is why,' he explained, 'you're called a mediator. You are supposed to be helping to bring these troubled souls to spiritual fulfillment—'

'Look, Father Dom,' I said. I tucked my oozing hands out of sight. 'I don't know what kind of ghosts you've been dealing with lately, but the ones I've been running into are about as likely to find spiritual fulfillment as I'm going to find a decent New York City-style slice of pizza in this town. It ain't gonna happen. These folks are going to hell or they're going to heaven or they're going on to their next life as a caterpillar in Kathmandu, but any way you slice it, sometimes they're gonna need a little kick in the butt to get them there . . .'

'No, no, no.' Father Dominic leaned forwards. He couldn't lean forwards too much because a week or so before, one of those troubled souls of his had decided to forego spiritual enlightenment and tried to snap his leg off instead. She also broke a couple of his ribs, gave him a pretty nifty concussion, tore up the school real good, and, let's see, what else?

Oh, yeah. *She tried to kill me.*

Father Dominic was back at school, but he was wearing a cast that went all the way down to his toes, and disappeared up his long black robe, who knew how far? Personally, I didn't like to think about it.

He was getting pretty handy with those crutches though. He could chase the late kids up and down the halls, if he had to. But since he was the principal, and it was up to the novices to hand out late slips, he didn't have to. Besides, Father Dom was pretty cool, and wouldn't do something like that even if he could.

Though he takes the whole ghost thing a little too seriously, if you ask me.

'Susannah,' he said tiredly. 'You and I, for better or for worse, were born with an incredible gift – ability to see and speak to the dead.'

'There you go again,' I said, rolling my eyes, 'with that *gift* stuff. Frankly, Father, I don't see it that way.'

How could I? Since the age of *two – two years old* – I've been pestered with, pounded on, *plagued* by restless spirits. For fourteen years, I've put up with their abuse, helping them when I could, punching them when I could not, always fearful of somebody finding put my secret and revealing me to be the biological freak I've always known I am, but have tried so desperately to hide from my sweet, long-suffering mother.

And then Mom remarried and moved me out to

3

California – in the middle of my sophomore year, thanks very much – where, wonder of wonders, I'd actually met someone cursed with the same horrible affliction: Father Dominic.

Only Father Dominic refuses to view our 'gift' in the same light as me. To him, it's a marvellous opportunity to help others in need.

Yeah, OK. That's fine for him. He's a *priest*. He's not a sixteen-year-old girl who, *hello*, would like to have a social life.

If you ask me, a 'gift' would have some plus side to it. Like superhuman strength or the ability to read minds, or something. But I don't have any of that cool stuff. I'm just an ordinary sixteen-year-old girl – well, OK, with above ordinary looks, if I do say so myself – who happens to be able to converse with the dead.

Big deal.

'Susannah,' he said now, very seriously. 'We are mediators. We aren't . . . well, *terminators*. Our duty is to intervene on the spirits' behalf, and lead them to their ultimate destination. We do that by gentle guidance and counselling, not by punching them in the face or by performing Brazilian voodoo exorcisms.'

He raised his voice on the word exorcisms, even though he knew perfectly well I'd only done the exorcism as a last resort. It's not my fault half the school fell down during it. I mean, technically, that was the ghost's fault, not mine.

'OK, OK, already,' I said, holding up both hands in an I-surrender sort of gesture. 'I'll try it your way from now on. I'll do the touchy-feely stuff. Jees. You West Coasters. It's all backrubs and avocado sandwiches with you guys, isn't it?'

Father Dominic shook his head. 'And what would you call your mediation technique, Susannah? Headbutts and choke-holds?'

'That's very funny, Father Dom,' I said. 'Can I go back to class how?'

'Not yet.' He puttered around with the cigarettes, tapping the pack like he was actually going to open it. That'll be the day. 'How was your weekend?'

'Swell,' I said. I held up my hands, knuckles turned towards him. 'See?'

He squinted. 'Good heavens, Susannah,' he said. 'What is *that*?'

'Poison oak. Good thing nobody told me it grows all over the place abound here.'

'It doesn't grow all over the place,' Father Dominic said. 'Only in wooded areas. Were you in a wooded area this weekend?' Then his eyes widened behind the lenses of his glasses. 'Susannah! You didn't go to the cemetery, did you? Not alone. I know you believe yourself to be indomitable, but it isn't all safe for a young girl like yourself to go sneaking around cemeteries even if you *are* a mediator.'

I put down my hands and said, disgustedly, 'I didn't catch this in any cemetery. I wasn't *working*. I got it at Kelly Prescott's pool party Saturday night.'

'Kelly Prescott's pool party?' Father Dominic looked confused. 'How would you have encountered poison oak there?'

Too late, I realized I probably should have kept my mouth shut. Now I was going to have to explain – to the principal of my school, who also happened to be a *priest*, no less – about how a rumour had gone around midway through the party that my step-brother Dopey and this girl named Debbie Mancuso were going at it in the pool house.

I had of course denied the possibility since I knew Dopey was grounded. Dopey's dad – my new stepfather, who, for a mostly laid-back, California kind of guy, had turned out to

5

be a pretty stern disciplinarian – had grounded Dopey for calling a friend of mine a fag.

So when the rumour went around at the party that Dopey and Debbie Mancuso were doing the nasty in the pool house, I was pretty sure everyone was mistaken. Brad, I kept insisting – everyone but me calls Dopey Brad, which is his real name, but believe me, Dopey fits him much better – was back home listening to Marilyn Manson through headphones, since his father had also confiscated his stereo speakers.

But then someone said, 'Go take a look for yourself,' and I made the mistake of doing so, tiptoeing up to the small window they'd indicated, and peering through it.

I had never particularly cared to see any of my step-brothers in the buff. Not that they are bad-looking or anything. Sleepy, the oldest one, is actually considered something of a stud by most of the girls at Junipero Serra Mission Academy, where he is a senior and I am a sophomore. But that doesn't mean I have any desire to see him strutting around the house without his boxers. And of course Doc, the youngest, is only twelve, totally adorable with his red hair and sticky-outy ears, but not what you'd call a babe.

And as for Dopey . . . well, I *particularly* never wanted to see Dopey in his altogether. In fact, Dopey is just about the *last* person on earth I'd ever wish to see naked.

Fortunately, when I looked through that window I saw that reports of my stepbrother's state of undress – as well as his sexual prowess – had been greatly exaggerated. He and Debbie were only making out. This is not to say that I wasn't completely repulsed. I mean, I wasn't exactly proud that my stepbrother was in there tongue wrestling with the second stupidest person in our class, after himself.

I looked away immediately of course; I mean, we've got

Showtime at home, for God's sake. I've seen plenty of French kissing before. I wasn't about to stand there gawking while my stepbrother engaged in it. And as for Debbie Mancuso, well, all I can say is, she ought to lay off the sauce. She can't afford to lose any more brain cells than she already has, what with all the hair spray she slathers on in the girls' room between classes.

It was as I was staggering away in disgust from the pool-house window, which was situated above a small gravel path, that I believe I stumbled into some poison oak. I don't remember coming into contact with plant life at any other time this past weekend, being a generally indoors kind of girl.

And let me tell you, I *really* stumbled into those plants. I was feeling light-headed from the horror of what I'd just seen – you know, the tongues and all – plus I had on my platform mules, and I sort of lost my balance. The plants I grabbed on to were all that saved me from the ignominy of collapsing on Kelly Prescott's redwood pool deck.

What I told Father Dominic, however, was an abridged version. I said I must have staggered into some poison oak as I was getting out of the Prescotts' hot tub.

Father Dominic seemed to accept this, and said, 'Well, some hydrocortisone ought to clear that up. You should see the nurse after this. Be sure not to scratch it or it will spread.'

'Yeah, thanks. I'll be sure not to breathe either. That'll probably be just about as easy.'

Father Dominic ignored my sarcasm. It's funny about us two both being mediators. I've never met anybody else who happened to be one – in fact, until a couple of weeks ago, I thought I was the only mediator in the whole wide world.

But Father Dom says there are others. He's not sure how many, or even how, exactly, we precious few happened to be picked for our illustrious – have I mentioned unpaid? – careers. I'm thinking we should maybe start a newsletter or something. *The Mediator News*. And have conferences. I could give a seminar on five easy ways to kick a ghost's butt and not mess up your hair.

Anyway, about me and Father Dom. For two people who have the same weird ability to talk to the dead, we are about as different as can be. Besides the age thing, Father Dom being sixty and me being sixteen, he's Mister Nice himself, whereas I'm . . .

Well, not.

Not that I don't try to be. It's just that one thing I've learned from all of this is that we don't have very much time here on earth. So why waste it putting up with other people's crap? Particularly people who are already dead, anyway.

'Besides the poison oak,' Father Dominic said. 'Is there anything else going on in your life you think I should know about?'

Anything else going on in my life that I thought he should know about. Let me see . . .

How about the fact that I'm sixteen, and so far, unlike my stepbrother Dopey, I still haven't been kissed, much less asked out?

Not a major big deal – especially to Father Dom, a guy who took a vow of chastity about thirty years before I was even born – but humiliating, just the same. There'd been a lot of kissing going on at Kelly Prescott's pool party – and some heavier stuff, even – but no one had tried to lock lips with me.

A boy I didn't know *did* ask me to slow dance at one point-though. And I said yes, but only because Kelly yelled at me after I turned him down the first time he asked. Apparently this boy was someone she'd had a crush on for a while. How my slow dancing with him was supposed to get him to like Kelly, I don't know, but after I turned him down the first time, she cornered me in her bedroom, where I'd gone to check my hair, and, with actual tears in her eyes, informed me that I had ruined her party.

'Ruined your party?' I was genuinely astonished. I'd lived in California for all of two weeks by then, so it amazed me that I had managed to make myself a social pariah in such a short period of time. Kelly was already mad at me, I knew, because I had invited my friends Cee Cee and Adam, whom she and just about everyone else in the sophomore class at the Mission Academy consider freaks, to her party. Now I had apparently added insult to injury by not agreeing to dance with some boy I didn't even know.

'Jesus,' Kelly said, when she heard this. 'He's a junior at Robert Louis Stevenson, OK? He's the star forward on their basketball team. He won last year's regatta at Pebble Beach, and he's the hottest guy in the Valley, after Bryce Martinsen. Suze, if you don't dance with him, I swear I'll never speak to you again.'

I said, 'All right already. What is your glitch, anyway?'

'I just,' Kelly said, wiping her eyes with a manicured finger, 'want everything to go really well. I've had my eye on this guy for a while now, and—'

'Oh, yeah, Kel,' I said. 'Getting me to dance with him is sure to make him like you.'

When I pointed out this fallacy in her thought process, however, all she said was, '*Just do it,*' only not the way they say it in Nike ads. She said it the way the Wicked Witch of the West said it to the winged monkeys when she sent them out to kill Dorothy and her little dog too.

I'm not scared of Kelly or anything, but really, who needs the grief?

So I went back outside and stood there in my Calvin Klein one-piece – with a sarong tied ever-so-casually around my waist – totally not knowing I had just stumbled into a bunch of poison oak, while Kelly went over to her dream date and asked him to ask me to dance again.

As I stood there, I tried not to think that the only reason he wanted to dance with me in the first place was that I was the only girl at the party in a swimsuit. Having never been invited to a pool party before in my life, I had erroneously believed people actually swam at them, and had dressed accordingly.

Not so, apparently. Aside from my stepbrother, who'd apparently become overwarm while in Debbie Mancuso's impassioned embrace and had stripped off his shirt, I was wearing the least clothes of anybody there.

Including Kelly's dream date. He sauntered up a few minutes later, wearing a serious expression, a pair of white chinos and a black silk shirt. Very Jersey, but then, this was the West Coast, so how was he to know?

'Do you want to dance?' he asked me in this really soft voice. I could barely hear him above the strains of Sheryl Crow, booming out from the pool deck's speakers.

'Look,' I said, putting down my Diet Coke. 'I don't even know your name.'

'It's Tad,' he said.

And then without another word, he put his arms around my waist, pulled me up to him, and started swaying in time to the music.

With the exception of the time I threw myself at Bryce Martinsen in order to knock him out of the way when a ghost was trying to crush his skull with a large chunk of wood, this was as close to the body of a boy – a *live* boy, one who was still breathing – I had ever been.

And let me tell you, black silk shirt not withstanding, I *liked* it. This guy felt *good*. He was all warm – it was kind of chilly in my bathing suit; being January, of course, it was supposed to be too chilly for bathing suits, but this *was* California, after all – and smelt like some kind of really nice, expensive soap. Plus he was just taller enough than me for his breath to kind of brush against my cheek in this provocative, romance novel sort of way.

Let me tell you, I closed my eyes, put my arms around this guy's neck, and swayed with him for two of the longest, most blissful minutes of my life.

Then the song ended.

Tad said, 'Thank you,' in the same soft voice he'd used before, and let go of me.

And that was it. He turned around, and walked back over to this group of guys who were hanging out by the keg Kelly's dad had bought for her on the condition she didn't let anybody drive home drunk, a condition Kelly was sticking strictly to, by not drinking herself and by carrying around a cellphone with the number of Carmel Cab on redial.

And then for the rest of the party, Tad avoided me. He didn't dance with anybody else. But he didn't speak to me again.

Game over, as Dopey would say.

But I didn't think Father Dominic wanted to hear about my dating travails. So I said, 'Nope. Nada. Nothing.'

'Strange,' Father Dominic said, looking thoughtful. 'I would have thought there'd be *some* paranormal activity—'

'Oh,' I said. 'You mean has any *ghost* stuff been going on?'

Now he didn't look thoughtful. He looked kind of annoyed. 'Well, yes, Susannah,' he said, taking off his glasses, and pinching the bridge of his nose between his thumb and forefinger like he had a headache all of a sudden. 'Of course, that's what I mean.' He put his glasses back on. 'Why? Has something happened? Have you encountered anyone? I mean, since that unfortunate incident that resulted in the destruction of the school?'

I said slowly, 'Well . . .'

Two

The first time she showed up, it was about an hour after I'd come home from the pool party. Around three in the morning, I guess. And what she did was, she stood by my bed and started screaming.

Really screaming. *Really* loud. She woke me out of a dead sleep. I'd been lying there dreaming about Bryce Martinsen. In my dream, he and I were cruising along Seventeen Mile Drive in this red convertible. I don't know whose convertible it was. His, I guess, since I don't even have my driver's licence yet. Bryce's soft wheat-coloured hair was blowing in the wind; and the sun was sinking into the sea, making the sky all red and orange and purple. We were going around these curves, you know, on the cliffs above the Pacific, and I wasn't even carsick, or anything. It was one really terrific dream.

And then this woman starts wailing, practically in my ear. I ask you: who needs that?

Of course I sat up right away, completely wide awake. Having a walking dead woman show up in your bedroom screaming her head off can do that to you. Wake you up right away, I mean.

I sat there blinking because my room was really dark – well, it was night-time. You know, night-time, when normal people are asleep.

But not us mediators. Oh, no.

She was standing in this skinny patch of moonlight coming in from the bay windows on the far side of my room. She had on a grey hooded sweatshirt, hood down, a T-shirt, capri pants and Keds. Her hair was short, sort of mousy brown. It was hard to tell if she was young or old, what with all the screaming and everything, but I kind of figured her for my mom's age.

Which was why I didn't get out of bed and punch her right then and there.

I probably should have. I mean, it wasn't like I could exactly yell back at her, not without waking the whole house. I was the only one in the house who could hear her.

Well, the only one who was alive, anyway.

After a while, I guess she noticed I was awake because she stopped screaming and reached up to wipe her eyes. She was crying pretty hard.

'I'm sorry,' she said.

I said, 'Yeah, well, you got my attention. Now what do you want?'

'I need you,' she said. She was sniffling. 'I need you to tell someone something.'

I said, 'OK. What?'

'Tell him . . .' She wiped her face with her hands. 'Tell him it wasn't his fault. He didn't kill me.'

This was sort of a new one. I raised my eyebrows. 'Tell him he *didn't* kill you?' I asked, just to be sure I'd heard her right.

She nodded. She was kind of pretty, I guess, in a waifish sort of way. Although it probably wouldn't have hurt if she'd eaten a muffin or two back when she'd been alive.

'You'll tell him?' she asked me, eagerly. 'Promise?'

'Sure,' I said. 'I'll tell him. Only who am I telling?'

She looked at me funny. 'Red, of course.'

Red? Was she *kidding?*

But it was too late. She was gone.

Just like that.

Red. I turned around and beat on my pillow to get it fluffy again. Red.

Why me? I mean, really. To be interrupted while having a dream about Bryce Martinsen just because some woman wants a guy named *Red* to know he *didn't* kill her . . . I swear, sometimes I am convinced my life is just a series of sketches for *America's Furniest Home Videos,* minus all that pants-dropping business.

Except my life really isn't all that funny if you think about it.

I especially wasn't laughing when, the minute I finally found a comfy spot on my pillow and was just about to close my eyes and go back to sleep, somebody else showed up in the sliver of moonlight in the middle of my room.

This time there wasn't any screaming. That was about the only thing I had to be grateful for.

'*What?*' I asked in a pretty rude voice.

He said, shaking his head, 'You didn't even ask her name.'

I leaned up on both elbows. It was because of this guy that I'd taken to wearing a T-shirt and boxer shorts to bed. Not that I had been going around in floaty negligees before he'd come along, but I sure wasn't going to take them up now that I had a male room-mate.

Yeah, you read that right.

'Like she gave me the chance,' I said.

'You could have asked.' Jesse folded his arms across his chest. 'But you didn't bother.'

'Excuse me,' I said, sitting up. 'This is *my* bedroom. I will treat spectral visitors to it any way I want to, thank you.'

He said, 'Susannah.'

He had the softest voice imaginable. Softer, even, than that guy Tad's. It was like silk or something, his voice. It was really hard to be mean to a guy with a voice like that.

But the thing was, I *had* to be mean. Because even in the moonlight, I could make out the breadth of his strong shoulders, the vee where his old-fashioned white shirt fell open, revealing dark, olive-complected skin, some chest hair, and just about the best defined abs you've ever seen. I could also see the strong planes of his face, the tiny scar in one of his ink-black eyebrows, where something – or someone – had cut him once.

Kelly Prescott was wrong. Bryce Martinsen was not the cutest guy in Carmel.

Jesse was.

And if I wasn't mean to him, I knew I'd find myself falling in love with him.

And the problem with that, you see, is that he's dead.

'If you're going to do this, Susannah,' he said, in that silky voice, 'don't do it halfway.'

'Look, Jesse,' I said. My voice wasn't a bit silky. It was hard as rock. Or that's what I told myself, anyway. 'I've been doing this a long time without any help from you, OK?'

He said, 'She was obviously in great emotional need, and you—'

'What about you?' I demanded. 'You two live on the same astral plane, if I'm not mistaken. Why didn't *you* get her rank and serial number?'

He looked confused. On him, let me tell you, confused looks good. *Everything* looks good on Jesse.

'Rank and what?' he asked.

Sometimes I forget that Jesse died a hundred and fifty or so years ago. He's not exactly up on the lingo of the twenty-first century, if you know what I mean.

'Her *name*,' I translated. 'Why didn't *you* get her name?'

He shook his head. 'It doesn't work that way.'

Jesse's always saying stuff like that. Cryptic stuff about the spirit world that I, not being a spirit, am still somehow expected to understand. I tell you, it burns me up. Between that and the Spanish – which I don't speak, and which he spouts occasionally, especially when he's mad – I have no idea what Jesse's saying about a third of the time.

Which is way irritating. I mean, I have to share my bedroom with the guy because it was in this room that he got shot, or whatever, in like 1850, back when the house had been a kind of hotel for prospectors and cowboys – or, as in Jesse's case, rich ranchers' sons who were supposed to be marrying their beautiful, rich cousins, but were tragically murdered on the way to the ceremony.

At least, that's what had happened to Jesse. Not that he's *told* me that or anything. No, I had to figure that out on my own . . . though my stepbrother Doc helped. It isn't something, it turns out, that Jesse seems much interested in discussing. Which is sort of weird because in my experience, all the dead ever want to talk about is how they got that way.

Not Jesse though. All he ever wants to talk about is how much I suck at being a mediator.

Maybe he had a point though. I mean, according to Father Dominic, I was supposed to be serving as a spiritual conductor between the land of the living and the land of the dead. But mostly all I was doing was complaining because nobody was letting me get any sleep.

'Look,' I said. 'I fully intend to help that woman. Just not now, OK? Now, I need to get some sleep. I'm totally wrecked.'

'Wrecked?' he echoed.

'Yeah. Wrecked.' Sometimes I suspect Jesse doesn't understand a third of what I'm saying either, though at least I'm speaking in English.

'Whacked,' I translated. 'Beat. All tuckered out. Tired.'

'Oh,' he said. He stood there for a minute, looking at me with those dark, sad eyes. Jesse has those kind of eyes some guys have, the kind of sad eyes that make you think you might want to try and make them not so sad.

That's why I have to make a point to be so mean to him. I'm pretty sure there's a rule against that. I mean, in Father Dom's mediation guidelines. About mediators and ghosts getting together and trying to, um, cheer each other up.

If you know what I mean.

'Goodnight, then, Susannah,' Jesse said, in that deep, silky voice of his.

'Goodnight,' I said. My voice isn't deep or silky. Right then, in fact, it sounded kind of squeaky. It usually does that when I'm talking to Jesse. Nobody else. Just Jesse.

Which is great. The only time I want to sound sexy and sophisticated, and I come out sounding squeaky. Swell.

I rolled over, bringing the covers up over my face, which I could tell was blushing. When I peeked out from underneath them a minute or so later I saw that he was gone.

That's Jesse's MO. He shows up when I least expect him to, and disappears when I least want him to. That's how ghosts operate.

Take my dad. He's been paying these totally random social calls on me since he died a decade ago. Does he show up when I really need him? Like when my mom moved me out here to a totally different coast and I didn't know anyone at first and I was totally lonely? Heck, no. No sign of good old Dad. He was always pretty irresponsible, but I'd really thought that the one time I'd need him . . .

I couldn't really accuse Jesse of being irresponsible though. If anything, he was a little *too* responsible. He had even saved my life, not once, but twice. And I'd only known him a couple of weeks. I guess you could say I kind of owed him one.

So when Father Dominic asked me, back in his office, whether or not any ghost stuff had been going on, I sort of lied and said no. I guess it's a sin to lie, especially to a priest, but here's the thing:

I've never exactly told Father Dom about Jesse.

I just thought he might get upset, you know, being a priest and all, to hear there was this dead guy hanging out in my bedroom. And the fact is, Jesse had obviously been hanging around the place for as long as he had for a reason. Part of the mediator's job is to help ghosts figure out what that reason is. Usually, once the ghost knows, he can take care of whatever it is that's keeping him stuck in that midway point between life and death, and move on.

But sometimes – and I suspected it was this way in Jesse's case – the dead guy doesn't *know* why he's still sticking around. He doesn't have the slightest idea. That's when I have to use what Father Dom calls my intuitive skills.

The thing is, I think I got sort of short-changed in this department because I'm not very good at being intuitive. What I'm a lot better at is when they – the dead – know perfectly well why they are sticking around but they just don't want to get to where they're supposed to go because what they've got in store there probably isn't that great. These are the worst kinds of ghosts, the ones whose butts I have no choice but to kick.

They happen to be my specialty.

Father Dominic, of course, thinks we should treat all ghosts with dignity and respect, without use of fists.

I disagree. Some ghosts just deserve to have the snot knocked out of them. And I don't mind doing it a bit.

Not the lady who'd showed up in my room though. She seemed like a decent sort, just sort of messed up. The reason I didn't tell Father Dom about her was that, truthfully, I was kind of ashamed of how I'd treated her. Jesse had been right to yell at me. I'd been a bitch to her, and knowing that he was right, I'd been a bitch to him too.

So you see, I couldn't tell Father Dom about either Jesse or the lady Red hadn't killed. I figured the lady I'd take care of soon, anyway. And Jesse . . .

Well, Jesse, I didn't know what to do about. I was pretty much convinced there wasn't anything I could do about Jesse.

I was also kind of scared I felt this way because I didn't really *want* to do anything about Jesse. Much as it sucked having to change clothes in the bathroom instead of in my room – Jesse seemed to have an aversion to the bathroom, which was a new addition to the house since he'd lived there – and not being able to wear floaty negligees to bed, I sort of liked having Jesse around. And if I told Father Dom about him, Father Dom would get all hot and bothered and want to help him get to the other side.

But what good would that do me? Then I'd never get to see him again.

Was this selfish of me? I mean, I kind of figured if Jesse wanted to go to the other side, then he would have done something about it. He wasn't one of those help-me-I'm-lost kind of ghosts like the one who'd shown up with the message for Red. No way. Jesse was more one of those don't-mess-with-me-I'm-so-mysterious kind of ghosts. You know the ones. With the accent and the killer abs.

So I admit it. I lied. So what? So sue me.

'Nope,' I said. 'Nothing to report, Father Dom. Supernatural or otherwise.'

Was it my imagination or did Father Dominic look a little disappointed? To tell you the truth, I think he sort of liked that I'd wrecked the school. Seriously. Much as he complained about it, I don't think he minded my mediation techniques so much. It certainly gave him something to get on a soapbox about, and as the principal of a tiny private school in Carmel, California, I can't imagine he really had all that much to complain about. Other than me, I mean.

'Well,' he said, trying not to let me see how let down he was by my lack of anything to report. 'All right, then.' He brightened. 'I understand there was a three-car pile-up out in Sunnyvale. Maybe we should drive out there and see if any of those poor lost souls need our aid.'

I looked at him like he was out of his mind. 'Father Dom,' I said, shocked.

He fiddled with his glasses. 'Yes, well . . . I mean, I just thought . . .'

'Look, *padre*,' I said, getting up. 'You gotta remember something. I don't feel the same way about this *gift* of ours that you do. I never asked for it and I've never liked it. I just want to be normal, you know?'

Father Dom looked taken aback. '*Normal?*' he echoed. As in, who would ever want to be *that?*

'Yes, *normal*,' I said. 'I want to spend my time worrying about the *normal* things sixteen-year-old girls worry about. Like homework and how come no boy wants to go out with me and why do my stepbrothers have to be such losers. I don't exactly relish the ghost-busting stuff, OK? So if they need me, let them find me. But I'm sure as heck not going looking for them.'

Father Dominic didn't get out of his chair. He couldn't

21

really, with that cast. Not without help. 'No boy wants to go out with you?' he asked, looking perplexed.

'I know,' I said. 'It's one of the wonders of the modern world. Me being so good-looking and all. Especially with these.' I raised my oozing hands.

Father Dominic was still confused though.

'But you're terribly popular, Susannah,' he said. 'I mean, after all, you were voted vice president of the sophomore class your first week at the Mission Academy. And I thought Bryce Martinsen was quite fond of you.'

'Yeah,' I said. 'He was.' Until the ghost of his ex-girlfriend – whom I was forced to exorcize – broke his collarbone, and he had to change schools, and then promptly forgot all about me.

'Well, then,' Father Dominic said, as if that settled it. 'You haven't anything to worry about in that category. The boy category, I mean.'

I just looked at him. The poor old guy. It was almost enough to make me feel sorry for him.

'Gotta get back to class,' I said, gathering my books. 'I've been spending so much time in the principal's office lately, people are gonna think I've got ties with the establishment and ask me to resign from office.'

'Certainly,' Father Dominic said. 'Of course. Here's your hall pass. And try to remember what we discussed, Susannah. A mediator is someone who *helps* others resolve conflicts. Not someone who, er, kicks them in the face.'

I smiled at him. 'I'll keep that in mind,' I said.

And I would too. Right after I'd kicked Red's butt.

Whoever he was.

Three

I found out who he was easily enough, it turned out. All I had to do was ask at lunch if anybody knew of a guy named Red.

Generally it's not that easy. I won't even tell you about the number of phone books I've scoured, the hours I've spent on the Internet. Not to mention the lame excuses I've had to make to my mother, trying to explain the phone bills I've racked up calling Information. 'I'm sorry, Mom. I just really had to find out if there was a store within a fifty-mile radius that carries Manolo Blahnik loafers . . .'

This one was so easy though it almost made me think, Hey, maybe this mediator stuff's not so bad.

That, of course, was then. I hadn't actually *found* Red at that point.

'Anybody know of a guy named Red?' I asked the crowd I had started eating lunch with, on what I guess was going to be a regular basis.

'Sure,' Adam said. He was eating Cheetos out of a family-size bag. 'Last name Tide, right? Enjoys killing harmless sea otters and other aquatic creatures?'

'Not that Red,' I said. 'This one is a human being. Probably adult. Probably local.'

'Beaumont,' Cee Cee said. She was eating pudding from

a plastic cup. A big fat seagull was sitting not even a foot way from her, eyeing the spoon each time Cee Cee dipped it back into the cup, then raised it again to her lips. The Mission Academy has no cafeteria. We eat outside every day, even, apparently, in January. But this, of course, was no New York January. Here in Carmel, it was a balmy seventy degrees and sunny outside. Back home, according to the Weather Channel, it had just snowed six inches.

I'd been in California almost three weeks, but so far it hadn't rained once. I was still waiting to find out where we were supposed to eat if it was raining during lunch.

I had already learned the hard way what happens if you feed the seagulls.

'Thaddeus Beaumont is a real estate developer.' Cee Cee finished up the pudding, and started on a banana she pulled from a paper bag at her hip. Cee Cee never buys school lunches. She has a thing about corn dogs.

Cee Cee went on, peeling her banana, 'His friends call him Red. Don't ask me why, since he doesn't have red hair. Why do you want to know, anyway?'

This was always the tricky part. You know the why-do-you-want-to-know? part. Because the fact is, except for Father Dom, no one knows about me. About the mediator thing, I mean. Not Cee Cee, not Adam. Not even my mother. Doc, my youngest stepbrother, suspects, but he doesn't *know*. Not all of it.

My best friend, Gina, back in Brooklyn, is probably the closest to having figured it out of anyone I know, and that's only because she happened to be there when Madame Zara, this tarot-card reader Gina had made me go to, looked at me with shock on her face and said, 'You talk to the dead.'

Gina had thought it was cool. Only she never knew – not really – what it meant. Because what it means, of course, is that I never get enough sleep, have bruises I can't explain given to me by people no one else can see, and, oh, yeah, I can't change clothes in my bedroom because the hundred-and-fifty-year-old ghost of this dead cowboy might see me naked.

Any questions?

To Cee Cee I just said, 'Oh, it's just something I heard on TV.' It wasn't so hard, lying to friends. Lying to my mother though, now *that* got a little sticky.

'Wasn't that the name of that guy you danced with at Kelly's?' Adam asked. 'You remember, Suze. Tad, the hunchback with the missing teeth and the terrible body odour? You came up to me afterwards and threw your arms around me and begged me to marry you so you'd be protected from him for the rest of your life.'

'Oh, yeah,' I said. 'Him.'

'That's his father,' Cee Cee said. Cee Cee knows everything in the world because she is editor – and publisher, chief writer and photographer – for the *Mission News*, the school paper. 'Tad Beaumont is Red Beaumont's only child.'

'Aha,' I said. It made a little more sense then. I mean, why the dead woman had come to me. Obviously, she felt a connection to Red through his son.

'What aha?' Cee Cee looked interested. Then again, Cee Cee always looks interested. She's like a sponge, only instead of water, she absorbed facts. 'Don't tell me,' she said, 'you've got it bad for that tool of a kid of his. I mean, what was that guy's problem? He never even asked your name.'

This was true. I hadn't noticed it either. But Cee Cee was right. Tad hadn't even asked my name.

Good thing I wasn't interested in him.

'I've heard bad things about Tad Beaumont,' Adam said, shaking his head. 'I mean, besides the fact that he's carrying around his undigested twin in his bowels, well, there's that embarrassing facial tick, controlled only by strong doses of Prozac. And you know what Prozac does to a guy's libido—'

'What's Mrs Beaumont like?' I asked.

'There's no Mrs Beaumont,' Cee Cee said.

Adam sighed. 'Product of divorce,' he said. 'Poor Tad. No wonder he has such issues about commitment. I've heard he usually sees three, four girls at a time. But that might be on account of the sexual addiction. I heard there's a twelve-step group for that.'

Cee Cee ignored him. 'I think she died a few years ago.'

'Oh,' I said. Could the ghost who'd shown up in my bedroom have been Mr Beaumont's deceased wife? It seemed worth a try. 'Anybody got a quarter?'

'Why?' Adam wanted to know.

'I need to make a call,' I said.

Four people in our lunch crowd handed me a cellphone. Seriously. I selected the one with the least intimidating amount of buttons, then dialled Information, and asked for a listing for Thaddeus Beaumont. The operator told me the only listing they had was for a Beaumont Industries. I said, 'Go for it.'

Strolling over to the monkey bars – the Mission Academy holds grades K through twelve, and the playground where we eat lunch comes complete with a sandbox, though I wouldn't touch it, what with the seagulls and everything – so I could have a little privacy, I told the receptionist who picked up with a cheerful, 'Beaumont Industries. How may I help you?' that I needed to speak to Mr Beaumont.

'Who may I say is calling please?'

I thought about it. I could have said, 'Someone who knows what really happened to his wife.' But the thing is, I

26

didn't really. I didn't even know why it was, exactly, that I suspected his wife – if the woman even was his wife – of lying, and that Red really had killed her. It's kind of depressing, if you think about it. I mean, me being so young and yet so cynical and suspicious.

So I said, 'Susannah Simon,' and then I felt lame. Because why would an important man like Red Beaumont take a call from Susannah Simon? He didn't know me.

Sure enough, the receptionist took me off hold a second later, and said, 'Mr Beaumont is on another call at the moment. May I take a message?'

'Uh,' I said, thinking fast. 'Yeah. Tell him . . . tell him I'm calling from the Junipero Serra Mission Academy newspaper. I'm a reporter, and we're doing a story on the . . . the ten most influential people in Salinas County.' I gave her my home number. 'And can you tell him not to call until after three? Because I don't get out of school till then.'

Once the receptionist knew I was a kid, she got even nicer. 'Sure thing, sweetheart,' she said to me in this sugary voice. 'I'll let Mr Beaumont know. Buh-bye.'

I hung up. Buh-bye bite me. Mr Beaumont was going to be plenty surprised when he called me back, and got the Queen of the Night People, instead of Lois Lane.

But the thing was, Thaddeus 'Red' Beaumont never even bothered calling back. I guess when you're a gazillionaire, being named one of the ten most influential people in Salinas County by a dinky school paper wasn't such a big deal. I hung around the house all day after school and nobody called. At least, not for me.

I don't know why I'd thought it would be so easy. I guess I'd been lulled into a false sense of security by the fact that I'd managed to get his name so easily.

I was sitting in my room, admiring my poison oak in the

dying rays of the setting sun, when my mom called me down to dinner.

Dinner is this very big deal in the Ackerman household. Basically, my mom had already informed me that she'd kill me if I did not show up for dinner every night unless I had arranged my absence in advance with her. Her new husband, Andy, aside from being a master carpenter, is this really good cook and had been making these big dinners every night for his kids since they grew teeth, or something. Sunday pancake breakfasts too. Can I just tell you that the smell of maple syrup in the morning makes me retch? What is wrong, I ask you, with a simple bagel with cream cheese, and maybe a little lox on the side with a wedge of lemon and a couple of capers?

'There she is,' my mom said, when I came shuffling into the kitchen in my after-school clothes: ripped-up jeans, black silk tee and motorcycle boots. It is outfits like this that have caused my stepbrothers to suspect that I am in a gang, in spite of my strenuous denials.

My mom made this big production out of coming over to me and kissing me on top of the head. This is because ever since my mom met Andy Ackerman – or Handy Andy as he's known on the cable home improvement show he hosts – married him, and then forced me to move to California with her to live with him and his three sons, she's been incredibly, disgustingly happy.

I tell you, between that and the maple syrup, I don't know which is more revolting.

'Hello, honey,' my mom said, smushing my hair all around. 'How did your day go?'

'Oh,' I said. 'Great.'

She didn't hear the sarcasm in my voice. Sarcasm has been completely wasted on my mother ever since she met Andy.

'And how,' she asked, 'was the student government meeting?'

'Bitchin'.'

That was Dopey, trying to be funny by imitating my voice.

'What do you mean, bitching?' Andy, over at the stove, was flipping quesadillas that were sizzling on this griddle thing he'd set out over the burners. 'What was bitching about it?'

'Yeah, Brad,' I said. 'What was bitching about it? Were you and Debbie Mancuso playing footsie underneath your desks or something?'

Dopey got all red in the face. He is a wrestler. His neck is as thick as my thigh. When his face gets red, his neck gets even redder. It's a joy to see.

'What are you talking about?' Dopey demanded. 'I don't even like Debbie Mancuso.'

'Sure, you don't,' I said. 'That's why you sat next to her at lunch today.'

Dopey's neck turned the colour of blood.

'David!' Andy, over by the stove, suddenly started yelling his head off. 'Jake! Get a move on, you two. Soup's on.'

Andy's two other sons, Sleepy and Doc, came shuffling in. Well, Sleepy shuffled. Doc bounded. Doc was the only one of Andy's kids who I could ever remember to call by his real name. That's because with red hair and these ears that stick out really far from his head, he looked like a cartoon character. Plus he was really smart, and in him I saw a lot of potential help with my homework, even if I was three grades ahead of him.

Sleepy, on the other hand, is of no use whatsoever to me, except as a guy I could bum rides to and from school with. At eighteen, Sleepy was in full possession of both his licence and a vehicle, a beat-up old Rambler with an iffy starter, but you were taking your life into your hands riding with him since he was hardly ever fully awake due to his night job as a pizza delivery boy. He was saving up, as he was fond of reminding us on the few occasions when he actually spoke, for a Camaro, and as near as I could tell, that Camaro was all he ever thought about.

'*She* sat by *me*,' Dopey bellowed. 'I do not like Debbie Mancuso.'

'Surrender the fantasy,' I advised him as I sidled past him. My mom had given me a bowl of salsa to take to the table. 'I just hope,' I whispered into his ear as I went by, 'that you two practised safe sex that night at Kelly's pool party. I'm not ready to be a stepaunt yet.'

'Shut up,' Dopey yelled at me. 'You . . . you . . . Fungus Hands!'

I put one of my fungus hands over my heart, and pretended like he'd stabbed me there.

'Gosh,' I said. 'That really hurts. Making fun of people's allergic reactions is so incredibly incisive and witty.'

'Yeah, dork,' Sleepy said to Dopey, as he walked by. 'What about you and cat dander, huh?'

Dopey, in out of his depth, began to look desperate.

'Debbie Mancuso,' he yelled, 'and I are not having sex!'

I saw my mom and Andy exchange a quick, bewildered glance.

'I should certainly hope not,' Doc, Dopey's little brother, said as he breezed past us. 'But if you are, Brad, I hope you're using condoms. While a good-quality latex condom has a failure rate of about two per cent when used as directed, typically the failure rate averages closer to twelve percent. That makes them only about eighty-five percent effective against preventing pregnancy. If used with a spermicide, the effectiveness improves dramatically. And condoms are our best defence – though not as good, of course, as abstention – against some STDs, including HIV.'

Everyone in the kitchen – my mother, Andy, Dopey, Sleepy and I – stared at Doc, who is, as I think I mentioned before, twelve.

'You,' I finally said, 'have way too much time on your hands.'

Doc shrugged. 'It helps to be informed. While I myself am not sexually active at the current time, I hope to become so in the near future.' He nodded towards the stove. 'Dad, your chimichangas, or whatever they are, are on fire.'

While Andy jumped to put out his cheese fire, my mother stood there, apparently, for once in her life, at a loss for words.

'I—' she said. 'I . . . Oh. My.'

Dopey wasn't about to let Doc have the last word. 'I am not,' he said, again, 'having sex with—'

'Aw, Brad,' Sleepy said. 'Put a sock in it, will ya?'

Dopey, of course, wasn't lying. I'd seen for myself that they'd only been playing tonsil hockey. Dopey and Debbie's fiery passion was the reason I had to keep slathering my hands with cortisone cream. But what was the fun of having stepbrothers if you couldn't torture them? Not that I was going to tell anyone what I'd seen, of course. I am many things, but not a snitch. But don't get me wrong: I would have liked Dopey to have gotten caught sneaking out while he was grounded. I mean. I don't think he'd exactly learned anything from his 'punishment'. He would still probably refer to my friend Adam as a fag the next time he saw him.

Only he wouldn't do it in my presence. Because, wrestler or not, I could kick Dopey's butt from here to Clinton Ave., my street back in Brooklyn.

But I wasn't going to be the one to turn him in. It just wasn't classy, you know?

'And did you,' my mother asked me, with a smile, 'feel that the student government meeting was as bitching as Brad seems to think it was, Suze?'

I sat down at my place at the dining table. As soon as I did so, Max, the Ackerman family dog, came snuffling along and put his head in my lap. I pushed it off my lap. He put it right back. Although I'd lived there less than a month, Max had already figured out that I am the person in the household most likely to have leftovers on my plate.

Mealtime was, of course, the only time Max paid attention to me. The rest of the time, he avoided me like the plague. He especially avoided my bedroom. Animals, unlike humans, are very perceptive towards paranormal phenomena, and Max sensed Jesse, and accordingly stayed far away from the parts of the house where he normally hung out.

'Sure,' I said, taking a sip of ice water. 'It was bitching.'

'And what,' my mother wanted to know, 'was decided at this meeting?'

'I made a motion to cancel the spring dance,' I said. 'Sorry, Brad. I know how much you were counting on escorting Debbie to it.'

Dopey shot me a dirty look from across the table.

'Why on earth,' my mother said, 'would you want to cancel the spring dance, Suzie?'

'Because it's a stupid waste of our very limited funds,' I said.

'But a dance,' my mother protested. 'I always loved going to school dances when I was your age.'

That, I wanted to say, is because you always had a *date*, Mom. Because you were pretty and nice and boys *liked* you.

32

You weren't a pathological freak, like I am, with fungus hands and a secret ability to talk to the dead.

Instead, I said, 'Well, you'd have been in the minority in our class. My motion was seconded and passed by twenty-seven votes.'

'Well,' my mother said. 'What are you going to do with the money instead?'

'Kegger,' I said, shooting a look at Dopey.

'Don't even joke about that,' my mother said sternly. 'I'm very concerned about the amount of teen drinking that goes on around here.' My mother is a television news reporter. She does the morning news on a local station out of Monterey. Her best thing is looking grave while reading off a Tele-PrompTer about grisly auto accidents. 'I don't like it. It isn't like back in New York. There, none of your friends drove, so it didn't matter so much. But here . . . well, everyone drives.'

'Except Suze,' Dopey said. He seemed to feel it was his duty to rub in the fact that although I am sixteen, I don't have a licence yet. Or even, for that matter, a learner's permit. As if driving were the most important thing in the world. As if my time was not already fully occupied with school, my recent appointment as vice president of the Mission Academy's sophomore class, and saving the lost souls of the undead.

'What are you *really* going to do with the money?' my mother asked.

I shrugged. 'We have to raise money to replace that statue of our founding father, Junipero Serra, before the Archbishop's visit next month.'

'Oh,' my mother said. 'Of course. The statue that was vandalized.'

Vandalized. Yeah, right. That's what everyone was going

around saying, of course. But that statue hadn't been vandalized. What had happened to it was, this ghost who was trying to kill me severed the statue's head and tried to use it as a bowling ball.

And I was supposed to be the pin.

'Quesadillas,' Andy said, coming over to the table with a bunch of them on a tray. 'Get 'em while they're hot.'

What ensued was such chaos that I could only sit, Max's head still on my lap, and watch in horror. When it was over every single quesadilla was gone, but my plate and my mom's plate were still empty. After a while, Andy noticed this, put his fork down and said, in an angry way, 'Hey, guys! Did it ever occur to you to wait to take seconds until everyone at the table had had their first serving?'

Apparently, it had not. Sleepy, Dopey and Doc looked sheepishly down at their plates.

'I'm sorry,' Doc said, holding his plate, cheese and salsa dripping from it, towards my mother. 'You can have some of mine.'

My mother looked a little queasy. 'No, thank you, David,' she said. 'I'll just stick with salad, I think.'

'Suze,' Andy said, putting his napkin on the table. 'I'm gonna make you the cheesiest quesadilla you ever—'

I shoved Max's head out of the way and was up before Andy could get out of his seat. 'You know what,' I said. 'Don't bother. I really think I'll just have some cereal, if that's OK.'

Andy looked hurt. 'Suze,' he said, 'it's no trouble—'

'No, really,' I said. 'I was gonna do my kick-boxing tape later anyway, and a lot of cheese'll just weigh me down.'

'But,' Andy said, 'I'm making more anyway . . .'

He looked so pathetic, I had no choice but to say, 'Well,

I'll try one. But for right now, finish what's on your plate, and I'll just go and get some cereal.'

As I was talking, I'd been backing out of the room. Once I was safely in the kitchen, Max at my heels – he was no dummy, he knew he wasn't going to get a crumb out of those guys in there: I was Max's ticket to people food – I got out a box of cereal and a bowl, then opened the fridge to get some milk. That was when I heard a soft voice behind me whisper, 'Suze.'

I whipped around. I didn't need to see Max slinking from the kitchen with his tail between his legs to know that I was in the presence of another member of that exclusive club known as the Undead.

Four

I nearly jumped out of my skin.

'Jees, Dad.' I slammed the fridge door closed. 'I told you not to do that.'

My father – or the ghost of my father, I should say – was leaning against the kitchen counter, his arms folded across his chest. He looked smug. He always looks smug when he manages to materialize behind my back and scare the living daylights out of me.

'So,' he said, as casually as if we were talking over lattes in a coffee shop. 'How's it going, kiddo?'

I glared at him. My dad looked exactly like he always had back when he used to make his surprise visits to our apartment in Brooklyn. He was wearing the outfit he'd been in when he died, a pair of grey sweatpants and a blue shirt that had *Homeport, Menemsha, Fresh Seafood All Year Round* written on it.

'Dad,' I said. 'Where have you been? And what are you doing here? Shouldn't you be haunting the new tenants back in our apartment in Brooklyn?'

'They're boring,' my dad said. 'Coupla yuppies. Goat cheese and cabernet sauvignon, that's all they ever talk about. Thought I'd see how you and your mom were getting on.' He was peering out of the pass-through Andy had put in when he was trying to update the kitchen from the 1850s-style decor that had existed when he and my mom bought it.

'That him?' my dad wanted to know. 'Guy with the – what is that anyway?'

'It's a quesadilla,' I said. 'And yeah, that's him.' I grabbed my dad's arm, and dragged him to the centre island so he couldn't see them any more. I had to talk in a whisper to make sure no one overheard me. 'Is that why you're here? To spy on Mom and her new husband?'

'No,' my dad said, looking indignant. 'I've got a message for you. But I'll admit, I did want to drop by and check out the lay of the land, make sure he's good enough for her. This Andy guy, I mean.'

I narrowed my eyes at him. 'Dad, I thought we'd been through all this. You were supposed to move on, remember?'

He shook his head, trying for his sad puppy-dog face, thinking it might make me back down. 'I tried, Suze,' he said woefully. 'I really did. But I can't.'

I eyed him sceptically. Did I mention that in life, my dad had been a criminal lawyer like his mother? He was about as good an actor as Lassie. He could do sad puppy-dog like nobody's business.

'Why, Dad?' I asked pointedly. 'What's holding you back? Mom's happy. I swear she is. It's enough to make you want to puke, she's so happy. And I'm doing fine, I really am. So what's keeping you here?'

He sighed sadly. 'You *say* you're fine, Suze,' he said. 'But you aren't *happy*.'

'Oh, for Pete's sake. Not that again. You know what would make me happy, Dad? If you'd move on. That's what would make me happy. You can't spend your afterlife following me around worrying about me.'

'Why not?'

'Because,' I hissed, through gritted teeth. 'You're going to drive me crazy.'

He blinked sadly. 'You don't love me any more, is that it, kiddo? All right, I can take a hint. Maybe I'll go haunt Grandma for a while. She's not as much fun because she can't see me, but maybe if I rattle a few doors—'

'Dad!' I glanced over my shoulder to make sure no one was listening. 'Look. What's the message?'

'Message?' He blinked, and then went, 'Oh, yeah. The message.' Suddenly, he looked serious. 'I understand you tried to contact a man today.'

I narrowed my eyes at him suspiciously. 'Red Beaumont,' I said. 'Yeah, I did. So?'

'This is not a guy you want to be messing around with, Suzie,' my dad said.

'Uh-huh. And why not?'

'I can't tell you why not,' my dad said. 'Just be careful.'

I stared at him. I mean, really. How annoying can you get? 'Thanks for the enigmatic warning, Dad,' I said. 'That really helps.'

'I'm sorry, Suze,' my dad said. 'Really, I am. But you know how this stuff works. I don't get the whole story, just . . . feelings. And my feeling on this Beaumont guy is that you should stay away. Far, far away.'

'Well, I can't do that,' I said. 'Sorry.'

'Suze,' my dad said. 'This isn't one you should take on alone.'

'But I'm not alone, Dad,' I said. 'I've got—'

I hesitated. Jesse, I'd almost said.

You would think my dad already knew about him. I mean, if he knew about Red Beaumont, why didn't he know about Jesse?

But apparently he didn't. Know about Jesse, I mean. Because if he had, you could bet I would have heard about it. I mean, come on, a guy who wouldn't get out of my bedroom? Dads hate that.

So I said, 'Look, I've got Father Dominic.'

'No,' my dad said. 'This one's not for him either.'

I glared at him. 'Hey,' I said. 'How do *you* know about Father Dom? Dad, have you been spying on me?'

My dad looked sheepish. 'The word *spying* has such negative connotations,' he said. 'I was just checking up on you, is all. Can you blame a guy for wanting to check up on his little girl?'

'Check up on me? Dad, how much checking up on me have you done?'

'Well,' he said, 'I'll tell you something. I'm not thrilled about this Jesse character.'

'*Dad!*'

'Well, whadduya want me to say?' My dad held out his arms in a so-sue-me gesture. 'The guy's practically living with you. It's not right. I mean, you're a very young girl.'

'He's deceased, Dad, remember? It's not like my virtue's in any danger here.' Unfortunately.

'But how're you supposed to change clothes and stuff with a *boy* in the room?' My dad, as usual, had cut to the chase. 'I don't like it. And I'm gonna have a word with him. You, in the meantime, are gonna stay away from this Mr Red. You got that?'

I shook my head. 'Dad, you don't understand. Jesse and I have it all worked out. I don't—'

'I mean it, Susannah.'

When my dad called me Susannah, he meant business.

I rolled my eyes. 'All right, Dad. But about Jesse. Please don't say anything to him. He's had it kind of tough, you know? I mean, he pretty much died before he ever really got a chance to live.'

'Hey,' my dad said, giving me one of his big, innocent smiles. 'Have I ever let you down before, sweetheart?'

Yes, I wanted to say. Plenty of times. Where had he been, for instance, last month when I'd been so nervous about moving to a new state, starting at a new school, living with a bunch of people I barely knew? Where had he been just last week when one of his cohorts had been trying to kill me? And where had he been Saturday night when I'd stumbled into all that poison oak?

But I didn't say what I wanted to. Instead, I said what I felt like I had to. This is what you do with family members.

'No, Dad,' I said. 'You never let me down.'

He gave me a big hug, then disappeared as abruptly as he'd shown up. I was calmly pouring cereal into a bowl when my mom came into the kitchen and switched on the overhead light.

'Honey?' she said, looking concerned. 'Are you all right?'

'Sure, Mom,' I said. I shovelled some cereal – dry – into my mouth. 'Why?'

'I thought—' My mother was peering at me curiously. 'Honey, I thought I heard you say, um. Well. I thought I heard you talking to— Did you say the word *dad?*'

I chewed. I was totally used to this kind of thing. 'I said bad. The milk in the fridge. I think it's gone bad.'

My mother looked immensely relieved. The thing is, she's caught me talking to Dad more times than I can count. She probably thinks I'm a mental case. Back in New York she used to send me to her therapist, who told her I wasn't a mental case, just a teenager. Boy, did I pull one over on old Doc Mendelsohn, let me tell you.

But I had to feel sorry for my mom, in a way. I mean, she's

40

a nice lady and doesn't deserve to have a mediator for a daughter. I know I've always been a bit of a disappointment to her. When I turned fourteen, she got me my own phone line, thinking so many boys would be calling me, her friends would never be able to get through. You can imagine how disappointed she was when nobody except my best friend, Gina, ever called me on my private line, and then it was usually only to tell me about the dates *she'd* been on. The boys in my old neighbourhood were never much interested in asking *me* out.

'Well,' my mom said brightly. 'If the milk's bad, I guess you have no choice but to try one of Andy's quesadillas.'

'Great,' I groaned. 'Mom, you do understand that around here, it's swimsuit season all year round. We can't just pig out in the winter like we used to back home.'

My mom sighed sort of sadly. 'Do you really hate it here that much, honey?'

I looked at her like she was the crazy one, for a change. 'What do you mean? What makes you think I hate it here?'

'You. You just referred to Brooklyn as "back home".'

'Well,' I said, embarrassed. 'That doesn't mean I hate it here. It just isn't home yet.'

'What do you need to make it feel that way?' My mom pushed some of my hair from my eyes. 'What can I do to make this feel like home to you?'

'God, Mom,' I said, ducking out from beneath her fingers. 'Nothing, OK. I'll get used to it. Just give me a chance.'

My mom wasn't buying it though. 'You miss Gina, don't you? You haven't made any really close friends here, I've noticed. Not like Gina. Would you like it if she came for a visit?'

I couldn't imagine Gina, with her leather pants, pierced tongue and extension braids, in Carmel, California, where wearing khakis and a sweater set is practically enforced by law.

I said, 'I guess that would be nice.'

It didn't seem very likely though. Gina's parents don't have very much money, so it wasn't as if they could just send her off to California like it was nothing. I would have liked to see Gina taking on Kelly Prescott though. Hair extensions, I was quite certain, were going to fly.

Later, after dinner, kick-boxing and homework, a quesadilla congealing in my stomach, I decided, despite my dad's warning, to tackle the Red problem one last time before bed. I had gotten Tad Beaumont's home phone number – which was unlisted, of course – in the most devious way possible: from Kelly Prescott's cellphone, which I had borrowed during our student council meeting on the pretence of calling for an update on the repairs of Father Serra's statue. Kelly's cellphone, I'd noticed at the time, had an address book function, and I'd snagged Tad's phone number from it before handing it back to her.

Hey, it's a dirty job, but somebody's got to do it.

I had forgotten to take into account, of course, the fact that Tad, and not his father, might be the one to pick up the phone. Which he did after the second ring.

'Hello?' he said.

I recognized his voice instantly. It was the same soft voice that had stroked my cheek at the pool party.

OK, I'll admit it. I panicked. I did what any red-blooded American girl would do under similar circumstances.

I hung up.

Of course, I didn't realize he had caller ID. So when the phone rang a few seconds later, I assumed it was Cee Cee, who'd promised to call with the answers to our Geometry homework – I'd fallen a little behind, what with all the

42

mediating I'd been doing . . . not that that was the excuse I'd given Cee Cee, of course – and so I picked up.

'Hello?' that same, soft voice said into my ear. 'Did you just call me?'

I said a bunch of swear words real fast in my head. Aloud, I only said, 'Uh. Maybe. By mistake though. Sorry.'

'Wait.' I don't know how he'd known I'd been about to hang up. 'You sound familiar. Do I know you? My name is Tad. Tad Beaumont.'

'Nope,' I said. 'Doesn't ring a bell. Gotta go, sorry.'

I hung up and said a bunch more swear words, this time out loud. Why, when I'd had him on the phone, hadn't I asked to speak to his father? Why was I such a loser? Father Dom was right. I was a failure as a mediator. A big-time failure. I could exorcize evil spirits, no problem. But when it came to dealing with the living, I was the world's biggest flop.

This fact was drilled into my head even harder when, about four hours later, I was wakened once again by a blood-curdling shriek.

Five

I sat up, fully awake at once.

She was back.

She was even more upset than she'd been the night before. I had to wait a real long time before she calmed down enough to talk to me.

'*Why?*' she asked, when she'd stopped screaming. 'Why didn't you *tell* him?'

'Look,' I said, trying to use a soothing voice, the way Father Dom would have wanted me to. 'I tried, OK? The guy's not the easiest person to get hold of. I'll get him tomorrow, I promise.'

She had kind of slumped down on to her knees. 'He blames himself,' she said. 'He blames himself for my death. But it wasn't his fault. You've got to tell him. *Please.*'

Her voice cracked horribly on the word *please*. She was a wreck. I mean, I've seen some messed up ghosts in my time, but this one took the cake, let me tell you. I swear, it was like having Meryl Streep put on that big crying scene from *Sophie's Choice* live on your bedroom carpet.

'Look, lady,' I said. Soothing, I reminded myself. Soothing.

There isn't anything real soothing about calling somebody *lady* though. So, remembering how Jesse had been kind of mad at me before for not getting her name, I went, 'Hey. What's your name anyway?'

Sniffling, she just went, 'Please. You've got to tell him.'

'I said I'd do it.' Jees, what'd she think I was running here? Some kind of amateur operation? 'Give me a chance, will you? These things are kind of delicate, you know. I can't just go blurting it out. Do you want that?'

'Oh, God, no,' she said, lifting a knuckle to her mouth, and chewing on it. 'No, please.'

'OK, then. Chill out a little. Now tell me—'

But she was already gone.

A split second later, though, Jesse showed up. He was applauding softly as if he were at the theatre.

'Now that,' he said, putting his hands down, 'was your finest performance yet. You seemed caring, yet disgusted.'

I glared at him. 'Don't you,' I asked grumpily, 'have some chains you're supposed to be rattling somewhere?'

He sauntered over to my bed and sat down on it. I had to jerk my feet over to keep him from squashing them.

'Don't you,' he countered, 'have something you want to tell me?'

I shook my head. 'No. It's two o'clock in the morning, Jesse. The only thing I've got on my mind right now is sleep. You remember sleep, right?'

Jesse ignored me. He does that, a lot. 'I had a visitor of my own not too long ago. I believe you know him. A Mr Peter Simon.'

'Oh,' I said.

And then – I don't know why – I flopped back down and pulled a pillow over my head.

'I don't want to hear about it,' I said, my voice muffled beneath the pillow.

The next thing I knew, the pillow had flown out of my

hands – even though I'd been clenching it pretty tightly – and slammed down to the floor. As hard as a pillow can slam, anyway, which isn't very hard.

I lay where I was, blinking in the darkness. Jesse hadn't moved an inch. That's the thing about ghosts, see. They can move stuff – pretty much anything they want – without lifting a finger. They do it with their minds. It's pretty creepy.

'*What?*' I demanded, my voice squeakier than ever.

'I want to know why you told your father that there's a man living in your bedroom.'

Jesse looked mad. For a ghost, he's actually pretty even tempered, so when he gets mad, it's really obvious. For one thing, things around him start shaking. For another, the scar in his right eyebrow turns white.

Things weren't shaking right then, but the scar was practically glowing in the dark.

'Uh,' I said. 'Actually, Jesse, there *is* a guy living in my bedroom, remember?'

'Yes, but—' Jesse got up off the bed and started pacing around. 'But I'm not really *living* here.'

'Well,' I said. 'Only because technically, Jesse, you're dead.'

'I *know* that.' Jesse ran a hand through his hair in a frustrated sort of way. Have I mentioned that Jesse has really nice hair? It's black and short and looks sort of crisp, if you know what I mean. 'What I don't understand is why you told him about me. I didn't know it bothered you that much, my being here.'

The truth is, it doesn't. Bother me, I mean. It used to, but that was before Jesse had saved my life a couple of times. After that, I sort of got over it.

Except it does bother me when he borrows my CDs and

doesn't put them back in the right order when he's done with them.

'It doesn't,' I said.

'It doesn't what?'

'It doesn't bother me that you live here.' I winced. Poor choice of words. 'Well, not that you *live* here, since . . . I mean, it doesn't bother me that you *stay* here. It's just that—'

'It's just that what?'

I said, all in a rush before I could chicken out, 'It's just that I can't help wondering *why*.'

'Why what?'

'Why you've stayed here so long.'

He just looked at me. Jesse has never told me anything about his death. He's never told me anything, really, about his life before his death either. Jesse isn't what you'd call real communicative, even for a guy. I mean, if you take into consideration that he was born a hundred and fifty years before *Oprah*, and doesn't know squat about the advantages of sharing his feelings, how not keeping things bottled up inside is actually good for you, this sort of makes sense.

On the other hand, I couldn't help suspecting that Jesse was perfectly in touch with his emotions, and that he just didn't feel like letting me in on them. What little I had found out about him – like his full name, for instance – had been from an old book Doc had scrounged up on the history of northern California. I had never really had the guts to ask Jesse about it. You know, about how he was supposed to marry his cousin, who it turned out loved someone else, and how Jesse had mysteriously disappeared on the way to the wedding ceremony . . .

It's just not the kind of thing you can really bring up.

'Of course,' I said, after a short silence, during which it

47

became clear that Jesse wasn't going to tell me jack, 'if you don't want to discuss it, that's OK. I would have hoped that we could have, you know, an open and honest relationship, but if that's too much to ask—'

'What about you, Susannah?' he fired back at me. 'Have you been open and honest with me? I don't think so. Otherwise, why would your father come after me like he did?'

Shocked, I sat up a little straighter. 'My dad came *after* you?'

Jesse said, sounding irritated, '*Nom de Dios*, Susannah, what did you expect him to do? What kind of father would he be if he didn't try to get rid of me?'

'Oh, my God,' I said, completely mortified. 'Jesse, I never said a word to him about you. I swear. He's the one who brought you up. I guess he's been spying on me, or something.' This was a humiliating thing to have to admit. 'So . . . what'd you do? When he came after you?'

Jesse shrugged. 'What could I do? I tried to explain myself as best I could. After all, it's not as if my intentions are dishonourable.'

Damn! Wait a minute though – 'You have *intentions*?'

I know it's pathetic, but at this point in my life, even hearing that the *ghost* of a guy might have intentions – even of the not dishonourable sort – was kind of cool. Well, what do you expect? I'm sixteen and no one's ever asked me out. Give me a break, OK?

Besides, Jesse's way hot, for a dead guy.

But unfortunately, his intentions towards me appeared to be nothing but platonic, if the fact that he picked up the pillow that he'd slammed on to the floor – with his hands this time – and smashed it in my face was any indication.

This did not seem like the kind of thing a guy who was madly in love with me would do.

'So what did my dad say?' I asked him when I'd pushed the pillow away. 'I mean, after you reassured him that your intentions weren't dishonourable?'

'Oh,' Jesse said, sitting back down on the bed. 'After a while he calmed down. I like him, Susannah.'

I snorted. 'Everybody does. Or did, back when he was alive.'

'He worries about you, you know,' Jesse said.

'He's got way bigger things to worry about,' I muttered, 'than me.'

Jesse blinked at me curiously. 'Like what?'

'Gee, I don't know. How about why he's still here instead of wherever it is people are supposed to go after they die? That might be one suggestion, don't you think?'

Jesse said quietly, 'How are you so sure this isn't where he's supposed to be, Susannah? Or me, for that matter?'

I glared at him. 'Because it doesn't work that way, Jesse. I may not know much about this mediation thing, but I do know that. This is the land of the living. You and my dad and that lady who was here a minute ago – you don't belong here. The reason you're stuck here is because something is wrong.'

'Ah,' he said. 'I see.'

But he didn't see. I knew he didn't see.

'You can't tell me you're happy here,' I said. 'You can't tell me you've *liked* being trapped in this room for a hundred and fifty years.'

'It hasn't been all bad,' he said, with a smile. 'Things have picked up recently.'

I wasn't sure what he meant by that. And since I was afraid my voice might get all squeaky again if I asked, I settled for saying, 'Well, I'm sorry about my dad coming after you. I swear I didn't tell him to.'

Jesse said softly, 'It's all right, Susannah. I like your father. And he only does it because he cares about you.'

'You think so?' I picked at the bedspread. 'I wonder. I think he does it because he knows it annoys me.'

Jesse, who'd been watching me pull on the chenille ball, suddenly reached out and seized my fingers.

He's not supposed to do that. Well, at least I'd been meaning to tell him he's not supposed to do that. Maybe it had slipped my mind. But anyway, he's not supposed to do that. Touch me, I mean.

See, even though Jesse's a ghost, and can walk through walls and disappear and reappear at will, he's still . . . well, *there*. To me anyway. That's what makes me – and Father Dom – different from everybody else. We not only can see and talk to ghosts, but we can feel them too – just as if they were anybody else. Anybody alive, I mean. Because to me and Father Dom, ghosts *are* just like anyone else, with blood and guts and sweat and bad breath and whatever. The only real difference is that they kind of have this glow around them – an aura, I think it's called.

Oh, and did I mention that a lot of them have superhuman strength? I usually forget to mention that. That's how come, in my line of work, I frequently get the you-know-what knocked out of me. That's also how come it kind of freaks me out when one of them – like Jesse was doing just then – touches me, even in a non-aggressive way.

And I mean, seriously, just because, to me, ghosts are as real as, say, Tad Beaumont, that doesn't mean I want to go around slow dancing with them or anything.

Well, OK, in Jesse's case, I would, except how weird would that be to slow dance with a ghost? Come on. Nobody but me'd ever be able to see him. I'd be like, 'Oh, let me introduce you to my boyfriend,' and there wouldn't be anybody there. How embarrassing. Everyone would think I was making him up like that lady on that movie I saw once on the Lifetime channel who made up an extra kid.

Besides, I'm pretty sure Jesse doesn't like me that way. You know, the slow dancing way.

Which he unfortunately proved by flipping my hands over and holding them up to the moonlight.

'What's wrong with your fingers?' he wanted to know.

I looked up at them. The rash was worse than ever. In the moonlight I looked deformed, like I had monster hands.

'Poison oak,' I said bitterly. 'You're lucky you're dead and can't get it. It bites. Nobody warned me about it, you know. About poison oak, I mean. Palm trees, sure, everybody said there'd be palm trees, but—'

'You should try putting a poultice of gum flower leaves on them,' he interrupted.

'Oh, OK,' I said, managing not to sound too sarcastic.

He frowned at me. 'Little yellow flowers,' he said. 'They grow wild. They have healing properties in them, you know. There are some growing on that hill out behind the house.'

'Oh,' I said. 'You mean that hill where all the poison oak is?'

'They say gunpowder works too.'

'Oh,' I said. 'You know, Jesse, you might be surprised to learn that medicine has advanced beyond flower poultices and gunpowder in the past century and a half.'

'Fine,' he said, dropping my hands. 'It was only a suggestion.'

'Well,' I said. 'Thanks. But I'll put my faith in hydrocortisone.'

He looked at me for a little while. I guess he was probably thinking what a freak I am. *I* was thinking how weird it was, the fact that this guy had held my scaly, poison-oaky hands.

Nobody else would touch them, not even my mother. But Jesse hadn't minded.

Then again, it wasn't as if he could catch it from me.

'Susannah,' he said finally.

'What?'

'Go carefully,' he said, 'with this woman. The woman who was here.'

I shrugged. 'OK.'

'I mean it,' Jesse said. 'She isn't – she isn't who you think she is.'

'I know who she is,' I said.

He looked surprised. So surprised it was kind of insulting, actually. 'You *know*? She *told* you?'

'Well, not exactly,' I said. 'But you don't have to worry. I've got things under control.'

'No,' he said. He got up off the bed. 'You don't, Susannah. You should be careful. You should listen to your father this time.'

'Oh, OK,' I said, very sarcastically. 'Thanks. Do you think maybe you could be creepier about it? Like could you drool blood or something too?'

I guess maybe I'd been a little *too* sarcastic, though, because instead of replying he just disappeared.

Ghosts. They just can't take a joke.

Six

'You want me to *what*?'

'Just drop me off,' I said. 'On your way to work. It's not out of your way.'

Sleepy eyed me as if I'd suggested he eat glass or something. 'I don't know,' he said slowly as he stood in the doorway, the keys to the Rambler in his hand. 'How are you going to get home?'

'A friend is coming to pick me up,' I said brightly.

A total lie, of course. I had no way of getting home. But I figured at a pinch, I could always call Adam. He'd just gotten his licence as well as a new VW bug. He was so hot to drive, he'd have picked me up from Albuquerque if I'd called him from there. I didn't think he'd mind too much if I called him from Thaddeus Beaumont's mansion on Seventeen Mile Drive.

Sleepy still looked uncertain. 'I don't know . . .' he said slowly.

I could tell he thought I was headed for a gang meeting or something. Sleepy has never seemed all that thrilled about me, especially after our parents' wedding when he caught me smoking outside the reception hall. Which is so totally unfair since I've never touched a cigarette since.

But I guess the fact that he'd recently been forced to

rescue me in the middle of the night when this ghost made a building collapse on me didn't exactly help form any warm bond of trust between us. Especially since I couldn't tell him the ghost part. I think he believes I'm just the type of girl buildings fall on top of all the time.

No wonder he doesn't want me in his car.

'Come on,' I said, opening up my camel-coloured calf-length coat. 'How much trouble could I get up to in this outfit?'

Sleepy looked me over. Even he had to admit I was the epitome of innocence in my white cable-knit sweater, red plaid skirt and penny loafers. I had even put on this gold cross necklace I had been awarded as a prize for winning this essay contest on the War of 1812 in Mr Walden's class. I figured this was the kind of outfit an old guy like Mr Beaumont would appreciate: you know, the sassy schoolgirl thing.

'Besides,' I said. 'It's for school.'

'All right,' Sleepy said at last, looking like he really wished he were someplace else. 'Get in the car.'

I hightailed it out to the Rambler before he had a chance to change his mind.

Sleepy got in a minute later, looking drowsy, as usual. His job, for a pizza stint, seemed awfully demanding. Either that or he just put in a lot of extra shifts. You would think by now he'd have saved enough for that Camaro. I mentioned that as we pulled out of the driveway.

'Yeah,' Sleepy said. 'But I want to really cherry her out, you know? Alpine stereo, Bose speakers. The works.'

I have this thing about boys who refer to their cars as 'she' but I didn't figure it would pay to alienate my ride. Instead, I said, 'Wow. Neat.'

We live in the hills of Carmel, overlooking the valley and the bay. It's a beautiful place, but since it was dark out all I could see were the insides of the houses we were driving by. People in California have these really big windows to let in all the sun, and at night-time when their lights are on you can see practically everything they're doing, just like in Brooklyn, where nobody ever pulled down their blinds. It's kind of homey, actually.

'What class is this for anyway?' Sleepy asked, making me jump. He so rarely spoke, especially when he was doing something he liked, like eating or driving, that I had sort of forgotten he was there.

'What do you mean?' I asked.

'This paper you're doing.' He took his eyes off the road a second and locked at me. 'You did say this was for school, didn't you?'

'Oh,' I said. 'Sure. Uh-huh. It's, um, a story I'm doing for the school paper. My friend Cee Cee, she's the editor. She assigned it to me.'

Oh my God, I am such a liar. And I can't leave at just one lie either. Oh, no. I have to pile it on. I am sick, I tell you. Sick.

'Cee Cee,' Sleepy said. 'That's that albino chick you hang out with at lunch, right?'

Cee Cee would have had an embolism if she'd heard anyone refer to her as a chick, but since, technically, the rest of his sentence was correct, I said, 'Uh-huh.'

Sleepy grunted and didn't say anything else for a while. We drove in silence, the big houses with their light-filled windows flashing by. Seventeen Mile Drive is this stretch of highway that's supposed to be like the most beautiful road in the world or something. The famous Pebble Beach Golf course is on Seventeen Mile Drive, along with about five other golf courses and a bunch of scenic points, like the Lone Cypress, which is some kind of tree growing out of a boulder, and Seal Rock, on which there are, you guessed it, a lot of seals.

Seventeen Mile Drive is also where you can check out the colliding currents of what they call the Restless Sea, the ocean along this part of the coast being too filled with riptides and undertows for anyone to swim in. It's all giant crashing waves and tiny stretches of sand between great big boulders on which sea gulls are always dropping mussels and stuff, hoping to split the shells open. Sometimes surfers get split open there, too, if they're stupid enough to think they can ride the waves.

And if you want, you can buy a really big mansion on a cliff overlooking all this natural beauty, for a mere, oh, zillion dollars or so.

Which was apparently what Thaddeus 'Red' Beaumont had done. He had snatched up one of those mansions, a really, really big one, I saw, when Sleepy finally pulled up in front of it. Such a big one, in fact, that it had a little guard's house by the enormous spiky gate in front of its long, long driveway, with a guard in it watching TV.

Sleepy, looking at the gate, went, 'Are you sure this is the place?'

I swallowed. I knew from what Cee Cee had said that Mr Beaumont was rich. But I hadn't thought he was *this* rich.

And just think, his kid had asked me to slow dance!

'Um,' I said. 'Maybe I should just see if he's home before you take off.'

Sleepy said, 'Yeah, I guess.'

I got out of the car and went up to the little guard's house. I don't mind telling you, I felt like a tool. I had been trying all day to get through to Mr Beaumont, only to be told he was in a meeting, or on another line. For some reason, I'd imagined a personal touch might work. I don't know what

I'd been thinking, but I believe it had involved ringing the doorbell and then looking winsomely up into his face when he came to the door.

That, I could see now, wasn't going to happen.

'Um, excuse me,' I said into the little microphone at the guard's house. Bulletproof glass, I noticed. Either Tad's dad had some people who didn't like him, or he was just a little paranoid.

The guard looked up from his TV. He checked me out. I saw him check me out. I had kept my coat open so he'd be sure to see my plaid skirt and loafers. Then he looked past me at the Rambler. This was no good. I did not want to be judged by my stepbrother and his crappy car.

I tapped on the glass again to direct the guard's attention back to me.

'Hello,' I said into the microphone. 'My name's Susannah Simon, and I'm a sophomore at the Mission Academy. I'm doing a story for our school paper on the ten most influential people in Carmel, and I was hoping to be able to interview Mr Beaumont, but unfortunately he hasn't returned any of my calls, and the story is due tomorrow, so I was wondering if he might be home and if he'd see me.'

The guard looked at me with a stunned expression on his face.

'I'm a friend,' I said, 'of Tad, Tad Beaumont, Mr Beaumont's son? He knows me, so if you want him, you know, to check me out on the security camera or whatever, I'm sure he could, you know, ID me. If my ID needs verifying, I mean.'

The guard continued to stare at me. You would think a guy as rich as Mr Beaumont could afford smarter guards.

'But if this is a bad time,' I said, starting to back away, 'I guess I could come back.'

Then the guard did an extraordinary thing. He leaned forwards, pressed a button, and said into the speaker, 'Honey, you talk faster than anyone I ever heard in my life. Would you care to repeat all that? Slowly, this time?'

So I said my little speech again, more slowly this time, while behind me, Sleepy sat at the wheel with the motor running. I could hear the radio blaring inside the car, and Sleepy singing along. He must have thought that his car was soundproof with the windows rolled up.

Boy, was he ever wrong.

After I was done giving my speech the second time, the guard, with a kind of smile on his face, said, 'Hold on, miss,' and got on this white phone, and started saying a bunch of stuff into it that I couldn't hear. I stood there wishing I'd worn tights instead of panty-hose since my legs were freezing in the cold wind that was coming in off the ocean, and wondering how I could ever have possibly thought this was a good idea.

Then the microphone crackled.

'OK, miss,' the guard said. 'Mr Beaumont'll see you.'

And then, to my astonishment, the big spiky gates began to ease open.

'Oh,' I said. 'Oh my God! Thank you! Thanks—'

Then I realized the guard couldn't hear me since I wasn't talking into the microphone. So I ran back to the car and tore open the door.

Sleepy, in the middle of a pretty involved air guitar session, broke off and looked embarrassed.

'So?' he said.

'So,' I said back to him, slamming the passenger door behind me. 'We're in. Just drop me off at the house, will you?'

'Sure thing, Cinderella.'

It took like five minutes to get down that driveway. I am not even kidding. It was *that* long. On either side of it were these big trees that formed sort of an alley. A tree alley. It was kind of cool. I figured in the daytime it was probably really beautiful. Was there anything Tad Beaumont didn't have? Looks, money, a beautiful place to live . . .

All he needed was cute little old me.

Sleepy pulled the car to a stop in front of this paved entranceway, which was flanked on either side by these enormous palm trees, kind of like the Polynesian Hotel at Disney World. In fact, the whole place had kind of a Disney feel to it. You know, really big, and kind of modern and fake. There were all these lights on, and at the end of all the paved stones I could see this giant glass door with somebody hovering behind it.

I turned to Sleepy and said, 'OK, I'm good. Thanks for the ride.'

Sleepy looked out at all the lights and palm trees and stuff. 'You sure you got a way home?'

'I'm sure,' I said.

'OK.' As I got out of the car, I heard him mutter, 'Never delivered a pie *here* before.'

I hurried up the paved walkway, conscious, as Sleepy drove away, that I could hear the ocean somewhere, though in the darkness beyond the house, I couldn't see it. When I got to the door, it swung open before I could look for a bell, and a Japanese man in black trousers and a white housecoat-looking thing bowed to me and said, 'This way, miss.'

I had never been in a house where a servant answered the door before – let alone been called miss – so I didn't know how to act. I followed him into this huge room where the walls were made out of actual rocks from which actual water was dripping in these little rivulets, which I guess were supposed to be waterfalls.

'May I take your coat?' the Japanese man said, and so I shrugged out of it, though I kept my bag from which my writing tablet was peeking out. I wanted to look the part, you know.

Then the Japanese man bowed to me again and said, 'This way, miss.'

He led me towards a set of sliding glass doors, which opened out on to a long, open-air courtyard in which there was a huge pool lit up turquoise in the dark. Steam rose from its surface. I guess it was heated. There was a fountain in the middle of it and a rock formation from which water gushed, and all around it were plants and trees and hibiscus bushes. A very nice place, I thought, for me to hang out in after school in my Calvin Klein one-piece and my sarong.

Then we were inside again in a surprisingly ordinary-looking hallway. It was at this point that my guide bowed to me for a third time and said, 'Wait here, please,' then disappeared through one of three doors off the corridor.

So I did as he said, though I couldn't help wondering what time it was. I don't wear a watch since every one I ever owned has ended up getting smashed by some evil spirit. But I hadn't planned on spending more than a few minutes of my time with this guy. My plan was to get in, deliver the dead lady's message, and then get out. I'd told my mom I'd be home by nine, and it had to be nearly eight by now.

Rich people. They just don't care about other people's curfews.

Then the Japanese man reappeared, bowed and said, 'He will see you now.'

Whoa. I wondered if I should genuflect.

I restrained myself. Instead, I went through the door – and

found myself in an elevator. A tiny little elevator with a chair and an end table in it. There was even a plant on the end table. The Japanese man had shut the door behind me, and now I was alone in a tiny room that was definitely moving. Whether it was going up or down, I had no way of knowing. There were no numbers over the door to indicate the direction the thing was taking. And there was only one button . . .

The room stopped moving. When I reached for the doorknob, it turned. And when I stepped out of the elevator, I found myself in a darkened room with big velvet curtains pulled over the windows, containing only a massive desk, an even more massive aquarium and a single visitor's chair, evidently for me, in front of that desk. Behind the desk sat a man. The man, when he saw me, smiled.

'Ah,' he said. 'You must be Miss Simon.'

Seven

'Um,' I said. 'Yes.'

It was hard to tell, because it was so dark in the room, but the man behind the desk appeared to be about my step-father's age. Forty-five or so. He was wearing a sweater over a button-down collared shirt, sort of like Bill Gates always does. He had brown hair that was obviously thinning. Cee Cee was right: it certainly wasn't red.

And he wasn't anywhere near as good-looking as his son.

'Sit down,' Mr Beaumont said. 'Sit down. I'm so delighted to see you. Tad's told me so much about you.'

Yeah, right. I wondered what he'd say if I pointed out that Tad didn't even know my name. But since I was still playing the part of the eager girl reporter, I smiled as I settled into the comfortable leather chair in front of his desk.

'Would you like anything?' Mr Beaumont asked. 'Tea? Lemonade?'

'Oh, no thank you,' I said. It was hard not to stare at the aquarium behind him. It was built into the wall, almost filling it up, and was stocked with every colour fish imaginable. There were lights built into the sand at the bottom of the tank that cast this weird, watery glow around the room. Mr Beaumont's face, with this wavy light on it, looked kind of Grand Moff Tarkinish. You know, in the final Death Star battle scene.

'I don't want to put you to any trouble,' I said in response to his question about liquid refreshment.

'Oh, it's no trouble at all. Yoshi can get it for you.' Mr Beaumont reached for the phone on the centre of his giant, Victorian-looking desk. 'Shall I ask him to get you anything?'

'Really,' I said. 'I'm fine.' And then I crossed my legs because I was still freezing from when I'd stood outside by the guard's house.

'Oh, but you're cold,' Mr Beaumont said. 'Here, let me light a fire.'

'No,' I said. 'Really. It's all . . . right . . .'

My voice trailed off. Mr Beaumont had not, as Andy would have done, stood up, gone to the fireplace, stuffed wadded up pieces of newspaper under some logs, lit the thing, and then spent the next half hour blowing on it and cursing.

Instead, he lifted up a remote control, hit a button, and all of a sudden this cheerful fire was going in the black marble fireplace. I felt its heat at once.

'Wow,' I said. 'That sure is . . . convenient.'

'Isn't it?' Mr Beaumont smiled at me. He kept looking, for some reason, at the cross around my neck. 'I never was one for building fires. So messy. I was never a very good Boy Scout.'

'Ha ha,' I said. The only way, I thought to myself, that this could get any weirder would be if it turns out he has that dead lady's head on ice somewhere in the basement, ready for transplantation on to Cindy Crawford's body as soon it becomes available.

'Well, if I could get straight to the point, Mr Beaumont—'

'Of course. Ten most influential people in Carmel, is it? And what number am I? One, I hope.'

He smiled even harder at me. I smiled back at him. It hate to admit it, but this is always my favourite part. There is definitely something wrong with me.

'Actually, Mr Beaumont,' I said, 'I'm not really here to do a story on you for my school paper. I'm here because someone asked me to get a message to you, and this is the only way I could think of to do it. You are a very hard person to get ahold of, you know.'

His smile had not faltered as I'd told him that I was there under false pretences. He may have hit some secret alarm button under his desk, calling for security, but if he did, I didn't see it. He folded his fingers beneath his chin and, still staring at my gold cross, said, 'Yes?' in this expectant way.

'The message,' I said, sitting up straight, 'is from a woman – sorry, I didn't get her name – who happens to be dead.'

There was absolutely no change in his expression. Obviously, I decided, a master at hiding his emotions.

'She said for me to tell you,' I went on, 'that you did not kill her. She doesn't blame you. And she wants you to stop blaming yourself.'

That triggered a reaction. He quickly unfolded his fingers, then flattened his hands out across his desk, and stared at me with a look of utter fascination.

'She said that?' he asked me eagerly. 'A dead woman?'

I eyed him uneasily. That wasn't quite the reaction I was used to getting when I delivered messages like the one I'd just given him. Some tears would have been good. A gasp of astonishment. But not this – let's face it – sick kind of interest.

'Yeah,' I said, standing up.

It wasn't just that Mr Beaumont and his creepy staring was freaking me out. And it wasn't that my dad's warning was ringing in my ears. My mediator instincts were telling me to get out, now. And when my instincts tell me to do something, I usually obey. I have often found it beneficial to my health.

'OK,' I said. 'Buh-bye.'

I turned around and headed back for the elevator. But when I tugged on the doorknob, it didn't budge.

'Where did you see this woman?' Mr Beaumont's voice, behind me, was filled with curiosity. 'This dead person?'

'I had a dream about her, OK?' I said, continuing to tug lamely on the door. 'She came to me in a dream. It was really important to her that you knew that she doesn't hold you responsible for anything. And now I've done my duty, so would you mind if I go now? I told my mom I'd be home by nine.'

But Mr Beaumont didn't release the elevator door. Instead, he said, in a wondering voice, 'You *dreamed* of her? The dead speak to you in your dreams? Are you a *psychic*?'

Damn, I said to myself. I should have known.

This guy was one of those New Agers. He probably had a sensory deprivation tank in his bedroom and burned aromatherapy candles in his bathroom and had a secret little room dedicated to the study of extraterrestrials somewhere in his house.

'Yeah,' I said, since I'd already dug the hole. I figured I might just as well climb in now. 'Yeah, I'm psychic.'

Keep him talking, I said to myself. Keep him talking while you find another way out. I began to edge towards one of the windows hidden behind the sweeping velvet curtains.

'But look, I can't tell you anything else, OK?' I said. 'I just had this one dream. About someone who seems like she might have been a very nice lady. It's a shame about her being dead and all. Who was she anyway? Your, um, wife?'

On the word *wife*, I pulled the curtains apart, expecting to find a window I could neatly put my foot through, then jump to safety. No biggie. I'd done it a hundred times before.

And there was a window there all right. A ten foot one with lots of individual panes, set back a foot, at least, in a nicely panelled casement.

But someone had pulled the shutters – you know, the ones that go on the outside of the house and are mostly just decorative – closed. Tightly closed. Not a ray of sunshine could have penetrated those things.

'It must be terribly exciting,' Mr Beaumont was saying behind me as I stared at the shutters, wondering if they'd open if I kicked them hard enough. But then who was to say what kind of drop lay below them? I could be fifty feet up for all I knew. I've made some serious leaps in my life, but I usually like to know what I'm leaping into before I go for it.

'Being psychic, I mean,' Tad's dad went on. 'I wonder if you would mind getting in touch with other deceased individuals I might know. There are a few people I've been longing to talk to.'

'It doesn't –' I let go of those curtains and moved to the next window – 'work that way.'

Same thing. The window was completely shuttered up. Not even a chink where sunlight might spill through. In fact, they looked almost nailed shut.

But that was ridiculous. Who would nail shutters over their windows? Especially with the kind of sea view I was sure Mr Beaumont's house afforded.

'Oh, but surely, if you really concentrated –' Mr Beaumont's pleasant voice followed me as I moved to the next window – 'you could communicate with just a few others. I mean, you've already succeeded with one. What's a few more? I'd pay you of course.'

66

I couldn't believe it. Every single one of the windows was shuttered.

'Um,' I said as I got to the last window and found it similarly shuttered. 'Agoraphobic much?'

Mr Beaumont must have finally noticed what I was doing since he said, casually, 'Oh, that. Yes. I'm sensitive to sunlight. So bad for the skin.'

Oh, OK. This guy was certifiable.

There was only one other door in the room, and that one was behind Mr Beaumont, next to the aquarium. I didn't exactly relish the idea of going anywhere near that guy, so I headed back for the door to the elevator.

'Look, can you please unlock this so I can go home?' I tugged on the knob, trying not to let my fear show. 'My mom is really strict, and if I miss my curfew, she . . . she might *beat* me.'

I know this was shovelling it on a bit thick – especially if he ever happened to watch the local news and saw my mother doing one of her reports. She is so not the abusive type. But the thing was, there was something so creepy about him, I really just wanted to get out, and I didn't care how. I'd have said anything to get out of there.

'Do you think,' Mr Beaumont wanted to know, 'that if I were very quiet, you might be able to summon this woman's spirit again so that I could have a word with her?'

'No,' I said. 'Could you please open this door?'

'Don't you wonder what she could have meant?' Mr Beaumont asked me. 'I mean, she told you to tell me not to blame myself for her death. As if I, in some way, were responsible for killing her. Didn't that make you wonder a little, Miss Simon? I mean, about whether or not I might be a—'

Right then, to my utter relief, the knob to the elevator

door turned in my hand. But not, it turned out, because Mr Beaumont had released it. No, it turned out somebody was getting out of the elevator.

'Hello,' said a blond man, much younger than Mr Beaumont, and dressed in a suit and tie. 'What have we here?'

'This is Miss Simon, Marcus,' Mr Beaumont said, happily. 'She's a psychic.'

Marcus, for some reason, kept looking at my necklace too. Not just my necklace, either, but my whole throat area.

'Psychic, eh?' he said, his gaze sweeping the neckline of my sweater. 'Is that what you two were discussing down here? Yoshi told me something about a newspaper article . . .'

'Oh, no.' Mr Beaumont waved a hand as if to dismiss the whole newspaper thing. 'That was just something she made up to get me to see her so she could tell me about the dream. Really quite an extraordinary dream, Marcus. She says she had a dream that a woman told her I didn't kill her. *Didn't* kill her, Marcus. Isn't that interesting?'

'It certainly is,' Marcus said. He took hold of my arm. 'Well, I'm glad you two had a nice little visit. Now I'm afraid Miss Simon has to go.'

'Oh, no.' Mr Beaumont, for the first time, stood up behind his desk. He was very tall, I noticed. He also had on green corduroy pants. Green!

Really, if you ask me, that was the weirdest thing of all.

'We were just getting to know one another,' Mr Beaumont said, mournfully.

'I told my mom I'd be home by nine,' I told Marcus really fast.

Marcus was no dummy. He steered me right into that elevator, saying, to Mr Beaumont, 'We'll have Miss Simon back sometime soon.'

'Wait.' Mr Beaumont started to come around from behind his desk. 'I haven't had a chance to—'

But Marcus jumped into the elevator with me and, letting go of me, slammed the door behind him.

Eight

A second later we were moving. Whether we were going up or down. I still couldn't tell. But it didn't really matter. The fact was, we were moving, and away from Mr Beaumont, which was all I cared about.

'Jees,' I couldn't help bursting out as soon as I knew I was safe, 'What is *with* that guy?'

Marcus looked down at me.

'Did Mr Beaumont hurt you in any way, Miss Simon?'

I blinked at him. 'No.'

'I'm very glad to hear that.' Marcus looked a little relieved, but he tried to cover it up by being businesslike. 'Mr Beaumont,' he said, 'is a little tired this evening. He is a very important, very busy man.'

'I hate to be the one to tell you this, but that guy's more than just tired.'

'Be that as it may,' Marcus said, 'Mr Beaumont does not have time for little girls who enjoy playing pranks.'

'*Prank?*' I echoed, mightily offended. 'Listen, mister, I really did . . .' What was I *saying?* 'I really did, um, have that dream, and I resent—'

Marcus looked down at me tiredly. 'Miss Simon,' he said, in a bored voice. 'I really don't want to have to call your parents. And if you promise me you won't bother Mr

Beaumont ever again with any more of this psychic dream business, I won't.'

I almost laughed out loud at that. My *parents*? I'd been worried he was set to call the *police*. My parents I could handle. The police were another matter entirely.

'Oh,' I said when the elevator stopped and Marcus opened the door and let me back out into the little corridor off the courtyard where they kept the pool. 'All right.' I tried to put a lot of petulant disappointment in my voice. 'I promise.'

'Thank you,' Marcus said.

He nodded, and then started walking me towards the front door.

He probably would have kicked me out without another thought if it hadn't been for the fact that as we were heading past the pool I happened to notice that someone was swimming laps in it. I couldn't tell who it was at first. It was really dark out, the night sky both moonless and starless because of a thick layer of clouds, and the only lights were the big round ones under the water. They made the person in it look all distorted – kind of like Mr Beaumont's face with the light from the aquarium all over it.

But then the swimmer reached the end of the pool and, his exercise regimen apparently complete, lifted himself out of it, and reached for a towel he'd thrown across a deck chair.

I froze.

And not just because I recognized him. I froze because really, it's not every day you see a *Greek god* right here on earth.

I mean it. Tad Beaumont in a bathing suit was a beautiful sight to see. In the blue light from the pool, he looked like an Adonis, with water sparkling all over the dark hair that coated his chest and legs. And if his abs weren't quite as impressive as Jesse's, well, at least he had a really buff set of biceps to make up for it.

'Hi, Tad,' I said.

Tad looked up. He'd been drying himself with the towel. Now he paused and looked me over.

'Oh, hey,' he said, recognizing me. A big smile broke out across his face. 'It's you.'

Cee Cee had been right. He didn't even know my name.

'Yeah,' I said. 'Suze Simon. From Kelly Prescott's party.'

'Sure, I remember.' Tad sauntered over to us, the towel slung casually over his shoulders. 'How you doin'?'

His smile was something to see, let me tell you. His dad had probably paid some orthodontist a pretty penny for it, but it was worth it, every cent.

'You know this young lady, Tad?' Marcus said, his disbelief evident in his tone.

'Oh, sure,' Tad said. He stood next to me, water still dripping from his dark hair like diamonds. 'We go way back.'

'Well,' Marcus said. And then he evidently couldn't think of anything to add to that, since he said it again. '*Well.*'

And then, after an awkward silence, he said it a third time, but then added, 'I guess I'll leave you two alone then. Tad, you'll show Miss Simon the way out?'

'Sure,' Tad said. Then, when Marcus had disappeared back through the sliding glass doors into the house, he whispered, 'Sorry about that. Marcus is a great guy, but he's kind of a worrier.'

Having met his boss, I didn't exactly blame Marcus for worrying. But since I couldn't say that to Tad, I just went, 'I'm sure he's very nice.'

And then I told him about the story I was doing for the school paper. I figured even if they discussed it later, his dad wasn't going to go, 'Oh, no *that's* not why she was here. She was here to tell me about this dream she had.'

And even if he did, he was so weird I doubt even his own son would believe him.

'Huh,' Tad said when I was through describing my article on the ten most influential people in Carmel. 'That's cool.'

'Yeah,' I babbled on. 'I didn't even know he was your dad.' God, I can lay it on when I try. 'I mean, I never did get your last name. So this is a real surprise. Hey, listen, can I borrow a phone? I've got to see about engineering a ride home.'

Tad looked down at me in surprise. 'You need a ride? No sweat. I'll take you.'

I couldn't help looking him up and down. I mean, he was practically naked and all. OK, well, not naked, since he was wearing a pair of swimming trunks that did reach practically to his knees. But he was naked enough for me not to be able to look away.

'Um,' I said. 'Thanks.'

He followed my gaze, and looked down at his dripping shorts.

'Oh,' he said, the beautiful smile going gorgeously sheepish. 'Let me just throw something on first. Wait here for me?'

And he took the towel from around his neck and started towards the back of his house—

But froze when I gasped and said, 'Oh my God! What's wrong with your *neck*?'

Instantly, he hunched his shoulders, and spun around to face me again. 'Nothing,' he said too fast.

'There most certainly is *not* nothing wrong with it,' I said, taking a step toward him. 'You've got some kind of horrible—'

And then, my voice trailing off, I dropped my gaze down towards my hands.

'Look,' Tad said uncomfortably. 'It's just poison oak. I know it's gross. I've had it for a couple of days. It looks worse than it is. I don't how I got it, especially on the back of my neck, but—'

'I do.'

I held up both my hands. In the blue glow from the pool lights, the rash on them looked particularly grotesque – just like the rash on the back of his neck.

'I tripped and fell into some plants the night of Kelly's party,' I explained. 'And right after that, you asked me to dance . . .'

Tad looked down at my hands. Then he started to laugh.

'I'm so sorry,' I said. I really felt bad. I mean, I had disfigured the guy. This incredibly sexy, fabulous-looking guy. 'Really, you don't know—'

But Tad just kept laughing. And after a while, I started laughing with him.

Nine

'Shuttered,' Father Dominic repeated. 'The windows were shuttered?'

'Well, not all of them,' I said. I was sitting in the chair across from his desk, picking at my poison oak. The hydrocortisone was drying it out. Now, instead of oozy, it was just plain scaly. 'Just the ones in his office, or whatever it was. He said he's sensitive to light.'

'And you say he kept staring at your neck?'

'At my necklace. It was his assistant who checked out my throat like he expected to see a giant hickey there, or something. But you're missing the point, Father Dom.'

I had decided to come clean with the good father. Well, at least about the dead woman who'd been waking me up in the middle of the night lately. I still wasn't ready to tell him about Jesse – especially considering what had happened when Tad had dropped me off the night before – but I figured if Thaddeus Beaumont Senior was actually the creepy killer I couldn't help suspecting he might be, I was going to need Father D's help to bring him to justice.

'The point,' I said, 'is that he was surprised for the wrong reason. He was surprised this woman had said he *hadn't* killed her. Which implies – to me anyway – that he really had. Killed her, I mean.'

Father Dominic had been working a straightened-out coat hanger underneath his cast when I'd walked in. Apparently he had an itch. He'd stopped scratching, but he couldn't let go of the piece of wire. He kept fingering it thoughtfully. But at least he hadn't gotten the cigarettes out yet.

'Sensitive to light,' he kept murmuring. 'Looking at your neck.'

'The point,' I said again, 'is that it seems like he really did kill this lady. I mean, he practically admitted it. The problem is, how can we prove it? We don't even know her name, let alone where she's buried – if anybody bothered burying her at all. We don't even have a body to point to. Even if we went to the cops, what would we say?'

Father D, however, was deeply absorbed in his own thoughts, turning the wire over and over in his hands. I figured if he was going to slip off into la-la land, well, then I would too. I sat back in my chair, scratching my poison oak, and thought about what had happened after Tad and I had got done laughing at each other's disfiguring rash – the only part of my evening I hadn't described to Father Dom.

Tad had gone and changed clothes. I had waited out by the pool, the steam rising from it warming my pantyhose-clad legs. Nobody bothered me, and it had actually been kind of restful listening to the waterfall. After a while, Tad reappeared, his hair still wet, but fully dressed in jeans and, unfortunately, another black silk shirt. He was even wearing a gold necklace, though I doubt he won his by writing a scintillating essay on James Madison.

It was all I could do not to point out that the gold was probably irritating his rash, and that black silk with jeans on a man is hopelessly Staten Island.

I managed to restrain myself, however, and Tad took me back inside, where Yoshi reappeared like magic with my coat. Then we went out to Tad's car, which I saw to my complete horror was some kind of sleek black thing that I swear to God David Hasselhoff drove on that show he did before *Baywatch*. It had these deep leather seats and the kind of stereo system that Sleepy would have killed for, and as I put my seat belt on, I prayed Tad was a good driver since I would die of embarrassment if anyone ever had to use the jaws of life to pry me from a car like that.

Tad, however, seemed to think the car was cool, and that in it, he was too. And I'm sure that in Poland, or somewhere, it *is* considered cool to drive a Porsche and wear necklaces and black silk, but at least back in Brooklyn if you did those things you were either a drug dealer or from New Jersey.

But Tad apparently didn't know that. He put the car in gear and an instant later, we were on the Drive, taking the hairpin curves along the coast as easily as if we were on a magic carpet. As he drove, Tad asked if I wanted to go somewhere, maybe get a cup of coffee. I guess now that we shared the common bond of poison oak, he wanted to hang.

I said sure, even though I hate coffee, and he let me use his cellphone to call my mother and tell her I'd be late. My mom was so thrilled to hear I was going somewhere with a boy, she didn't even do the usual things mothers do when their daughters are out with a boy they don't know, like demand his mother's name and home phone number.

I hung up, and we went to the Coffee Clutch, a particularly favourite haunt of kids from the Mission Academy. Cee Cee and Adam, it turned out, were there, but when they saw me come in with a boy, they tactfully pretended not to know me. At least, Cee Cee did. Adam kept looking over and making rude faces whenever Tad's back was turned. I don't know if the faces were due to the fact that Tad's rash was plainly evident even in the Coffee Clutch's dim lighting, or if Adam was just expressing his personal feelings over Tad Beaumont in general.

In any case, after two cappuccinos – for him – and two hot ciders for me, we left, and Tad drove me home. He wasn't, I'd discovered, a particularly bright guy. He talked an awful lot about basketball. When he wasn't talking about basketball, he was talking about sailing, and when he wasn't talking about sailing, he was talking about jet-skiing.

And suffice it to say, I know nothing about basket-ball, sailing or jet-skiing.

But he seemed like a decent enough guy. And unlike his father, he was clearly not nuts, always a positive. And he was, of course, devastatingly good-looking, so all in all, I would have rated the evening around a seven or eight, on a one to ten scale, one being lousy, ten being sublime.

And then, as I was undoing my seat belt after having said goodnight, Tad suddenly leaned over, took my chin in his hand, turned my face towards him, and kissed me.

My first kiss. Ever.

I know it's hard to believe. I'm so vibrant and bubbly and all, you would think boys had been flocking to me like bees to honey all my life.

Let's just say that's not exactly what happened. I like to blame the fact that I am a biological freak – being able to communicate with the dead and all – for the fact that I have never once been on a date, but I know that's not really it. I'm just not the kind of girl guys think about asking out. Well, maybe they think about it, but they always seem to manage to talk themselves out of it. I don't know if it's because they think I might ram a fist down their throat if they try anything, or if it's just because they are intimidated by my superior intelligence and good looks (ha ha). In the end, they just aren't interested.

Until Tad, that is. Tad was interested. Tad was *very* interested.

Tad was expressing his interest by deepening our kiss from just a little goodnight one to a fully fledged French – which I was enjoying immensely, by the way, in spite of the necklace and the silk shirt – when I happened to notice – yeah, OK. I'll admit it. My eyes were open. Hey, it was my first kiss, I wasn't going to miss anything, OK? – that there was somebody sitting in the Porsche's tiny little back seat.

I pulled my head away and let out a little scream.

Tad blinked at me in confusion.

'What's wrong?' he asked.

'Oh, please,' said the person in the back seat, pleasantly. 'Don't stop on my account.'

I looked at Tad. 'I gotta go,' I said. 'Sorry.'

And I practically flew out of that car.

I was barrelling up the driveway to my house, my cheeks on fire with embarrassment, when Jesse caught up to me. He wasn't even walking fast. He was just strolling along.

And he actually had the nerve to say, 'It's your own fault.'

'How is it *my* fault?' I demanded, as Tad, after hesitating a moment, started backing out of our driveway.

'You shouldn't,' Jesse said, calmly, 'have let him get so forward.'

'*Forward?* What are you *talking* about? *Forward?* What does that even *mean?*'

'You hardly know him,' Jesse said. 'And you were letting him—'

I whirled around to face him. Fortunately, by that time, Tad was gone. Otherwise, he would have seen me, in the glow of his headlights, twirling around in my driveway, yelling at the moon, which had finally broken through the clouds.

'Oh, no,' I said, loudly. 'Don't even *go* there, Jesse.'

'Well,' Jesse said. In the moonlight, I could see that his expression was one of stubborn determination. The stubbornness was no mystery – Jesse was just about the stubbornest person I had ever met – but what he was so determined about, except maybe ruining my life, I couldn't figure out. 'You were.'

'*We were just saying goodnight,*' I hissed at him.

'I may have been dead for the past hundred and fifty years, Susannah,' Jesse said, 'but that doesn't mean I don't know how people say goodnight. And generally, when people say goodnight, they keep their tongues to themselves.'

'Oh, my God,' I said. I turned away from him, and started heading back towards the house. 'Oh, my God. He did *not* just say that.'

'Yes, I did just say that.' Jesse followed me. 'I know what I saw, Susannah.'

'You know what you sound like?' I asked him, turning around at the bottom of the steps to the front porch to face him. 'You sound like a jealous boyfriend.'

'*Nombre de Dios.* I am not,' Jesse said with a laugh, 'jealous of that—'

'Oh, yeah? Then where's all this hostility coming from? Tad never did anything to you.'

'Tad,' Jesse said, 'is a . . .'

And then he said a word I couldn't understand, because it was in Spanish.

I stared at him. 'A what?'

He said the word again.

'Look,' I said. 'Speak English.'

'There is no English translation,' Jesse said, setting his jaw, 'for that word.'

'Well,' I said. 'Keep it to yourself then.'

'He's no good for you,' Jesse said, as if that settled the matter.

'You don't even *know* him.'

'I know enough. I know you didn't listen to me or to your father when you went off tonight by yourself to that man's house.'

'Right,' I said. 'And I'll admit, it was very, very creepy. But Tad brought me home. Tad's not the problem there. His dad's the one who is a freak, not Tad.'

'The problem here,' Jesse said, shaking his head, 'is you, Susannah. You think you don't need anyone, that you can handle everything on your own.'

'I hate to break it to you, Jesse,' I said, 'but I *can* handle everything on my own.' Then I remembered Heather, the ghost of the girl who'd almost killed me the week before. 'Well, most everything,' I corrected myself.

'Ah,' Jesse said. 'See? You admit it. Susannah, this one – you need to ask the priest for help.'

'*Fine*,' I said. 'I will.'

'*Fine*,' he said. 'You had better.'

We were so mad at each other, and had been standing there yelling so hard, our faces ended up only a few inches apart. For a split second, I stared up at Jesse, and even though I was totally mad at him, I wasn't thinking about what a self-righteous jerk he is.

Instead, I was thinking about this movie I saw once where the hero caught the heroine kissing another man, and so he grabbed her and looked down at her all passionately and said, 'If kisses were what you were looking for, little fool, why didn't you come to me?'

And then he laughed this evil laugh and started kissing her.

Maybe, I couldn't help thinking, Jesse would do that, only

he'd call me *querida*, like he does sometimes when he's not all mad at me for Frenching guys in cars.

And so I sort of closed my eyes, and let my mouth get all relaxed, you know, in case he decided to stick his tongue in there.

But all that happened was that the screen door slammed, and when I opened my eyes, Jesse was gone.

Instead, Doc was there standing on the front porch looking down at me, eating an ice-cream sandwich.

'Hey,' Doc said, between licks. 'What are you doing out here? And who were you yelling at? I could hear you all the way inside. I'm trying to watch *Nova*, you know.'

Furious – but at myself more than anybody – I said, 'Nobody,' and stalked up the stairs and into the house.

Which was why the next day, I'd come to Father Dom's office first thing, and spilled my guts. No way was Jesse getting away with accusing me of thinking I don't need anyone. I need a lot of people.

And a boyfriend would be number one on that list, thank you very much.

'Sensitive to light,' Father Dominic said, coming out of his thoughtful reverie. 'His nickname is Red, but he doesn't have red hair. He was looking at your neck.' Father Dom opened the top drawer of his desk and took out his crumpled, unopened pack of cigarettes. 'Don't you see, Susannah?' he asked me.

'Sure,' I said. 'He's a whacko.'

'I don't think so,' Father Dom said. 'I think he's a vampire.'

Ten

I gaped at him.

'Uh, Father D?' I said after a while. 'No offence, but have you taken too many of your pain pills or something? Because I hate to be the one to break it to you, but there's no such thing as vampires.'

Father Dom looked closer than I'd ever seen him to ripping that pack open and popping one of those cigarettes into his mouth. He restrained himself however.

'How,' he asked, 'do you know?'

'How do I know what?' I demanded. 'That there's no such thing as vampires? Um, the same way I know there's no Easter Bunny or Tooth Fairy.'

Father Dominic said, 'Ah, but people say that about ghosts. And you and I both know that that's not true.'

'Yeah,' I said, 'but I've *seen* ghosts. I've never seen a vampire. And I've hung out in a lot of cemeteries.'

Father Dominic said, 'Well, not to state the obvious, Susannah, but I've been around a good deal longer than you have and while I myself have never before encountered a vampire, I am at least willing to concede the possibility of such a creature existing.'

'Yeah,' I said. 'OK, Father D. Let's just go out on a limb here and say the guy's a vampire. Red Beaumont is a very

83

high-profile guy. If he was going to go running around after dark biting people on the neck, somebody would notice, don't you think?'

'Not,' Father Dominic said, 'if he has, like you said, employees who are eager to protect him.'

This was too much. I said, 'OK. This has gotten a little too Stephen King for me. I gotta get back to class or Mr Walden's going to think I'm AWOL. But if I get a note from you later saying I'm gonna have to stake this guy in the heart, all bets are off. Tad Beaumont will so totally not ask me to the prom if I kill his dad.'

Father Dominic put the cigarettes aside. 'This,' he said, 'is going to take some researching . . .'

I left Father Dominic doing what he loved best, which was surfing the Net. The Mission's administrative offices had only recently gotten computers, and no one there really knew how to use them very well. Father Dominic in particular had no idea how a mouse worked, and was constantly sweeping it from one side of his desk to the other, no matter how many times I told him all he had to do was keep it on the mouse pad. It would have been cute if it hadn't been so frustrating.

I decided, as I walked down the breezeway, that I would have to get Cee Cee on the job. She was a little more adept at surfing the Web than Father Dominic.

As I approached Mr Walden's classroom – which last week had unfortunately received the brunt of the damage in what everyone had assumed was a freak earthquake, but which had actually been an exorcism gone awry – I noticed, standing to one side of the pile of rubble that had once been a decorative arch, a little boy.

It wasn't unusual to see very little kids hanging around the halls of the Mission Academy since the school had classes from kindergarten all the way up to twelfth grade. What was unusual about this kid, however, was that he was glowing a little.

And also, the construction workers who were swarming around trying to put the breezeway back up occasionally walked right through him.

He looked up at me as I approached, as if he'd been waiting for me. Which, in fact, he had been.

'Hey,' he said.

'Hi,' I said. The workmen were playing the radio pretty loud, so fortunately none of them noticed the weird girl standing there talking to herself.

'You the mediator?' the kid wanted to know.

'One of them,' I said.

'Good. I got a problem.'

I looked down at him. He couldn't have been more than nine or ten years old. Then I remembered that the other day at lunch, the Mission's bells had rung out nine times, and Cee Cee had explained it was because one of the third graders had died after a long bout with cancer. You couldn't tell it to look at the kid – the dead I encounter never wear outward signs of the cause of their death, assuming instead the form in which they'd lived before whatever illness or accident had taken their lives – but this little guy had apparently had a wicked case of leukemia. Timothy, I thought Cee Cee had said his name was.

'You're Timothy,' I said.

'Tim,' he corrected me, making a face.

'Sorry. What can I do for you?'

Timothy, all business, said, 'It's about my cat.'

I nodded. 'Of course. What about your cat?'

'My mom doesn't want him around,' Timothy said. For a

dead kid, he was surprisingly straightforward. 'Every time she sees him, he reminds her of me so she starts crying.'

'I see,' I said. 'Would you like me to find your cat another home?'

'That's the basic idea,' Timothy said.

I was thinking that about the last thing I wanted to deal with right then was finding some mangy cat a new home, but I smiled gamely and said, 'No problem.'

'Great,' Timothy said. 'There's just one catch . . .'

Which was how, after school that day, I found myself standing in a field behind the Carmel Valley mall, yelling, 'Here, kitty, kitty, kitty!'

Adam, whose help – and car – I'd enlisted, was the one beating the tall yellow grass since I'd shown him my poison-oaky hands and explained that I could not possibly be expected to venture anywhere near vegetation. He straightened, lifted a hand to wipe the sweat from his forehead – the sun was beaming down hard enough to make me long for the beach with its cool ocean breezes and, more importantly, totally hot lifeguards – and said, 'OK. I get that it's important that we find this dead kid's cat. But why are we looking for it in a field? Wouldn't it be smarter to look for it at the kid's house?'

'No,' I said. 'Timothy's father couldn't stand listening to his wife cry every time she saw the cat, so he just packed it up in the car and dumped it out here.'

'Nice of him,' Adam said. 'A real animal lover. I suppose it would have been too much trouble to take the cat to the animal shelter where someone might have adopted it.'

'Apparently,' I said, 'there isn't a whole lot of chance of anybody adopting this cat.' I cleared my throat. 'It might be a good idea for us to call him by his name. Maybe he'd come then.'

'OK.' Adam pulled up his chinos. 'What's his name?'

'Um,' I said. 'Spike.'

'Spike.' Adam looked heavenwards. 'A cat called Spike. This I can't wait to see. Here, Spike. Here, Spikey, Spikey, Spikey . . .'

'Hey, you guys.' Cee Cee came towards us waving her laptop in the air.

I'd enlisted Cee Cee's help as well as Adam's, only with a project of a different nature. All of my new friends, I'd discovered, had different talents and abilities. Adam's lay primarily in the fact that he owned a car, but Cee Cee's strengths lay in her superlative research skills . . . and what's more, in the fact that she actually *liked* looking stuff up. I'd asked her to look up what she could on Thaddeus Beaumont Senior, and she'd obliged. She'd been sitting in the car cruising the Net with the help of the remote modem she'd gotten for her birthday – have I mentioned that everyone in Carmel, with the exception of myself, is way rich? – while Adam and I looked for Timothy's cat.

'Hey,' Cee Cee said. 'Get a load of this.' She skimmed something she'd downloaded. 'I ran the name Thaddeus Beaumont through a search engine, and came up with dozens of hits. Thaddeus Beaumont is listed as CEO, partner or investor in over thirty land-development projects – most of which, by the way, are commercial ventures, like cineplexes, strip malls or health clubs – on the Monterey peninsula alone.'

'What does that mean?' Adam asked.

'It means that if you add up the number of acres owned by companies who list Thaddeus Beaumont as either an investor or a partner, he becomes roughly the largest land owner in northern California.'

'Wow,' I said. I was thinking about the prom. I bet a guy

87

who owned that much land could afford to rent his son a stretch limo for the night. Dorky, I know, but I'd always wanted to ride in one.

'But he doesn't really own all that land,' Adam pointed out. 'The companies do.'

'Exactly,' Cee Cee said.

'Exactly what do you mean by exactly?'

'Well,' Cee Cee said. 'Just that it might explain why it is that the guy hasn't been hauled into court for suspicion of murder.'

'Murder?' Suddenly, I forgot all about prom. 'What about a murder?'

'*A* murder?' Cee Cee spun her laptop around so that we could see the screen. 'We're talking multiple murders. Although technically, the victims have all been listed only as missing.'

'What are you *talking* about?'

'Well, after I made a list of all of the companies affiliated with Thaddeus Beaumont, I entered each company name into that same search engine and came up with a couple of pretty disturbing things. Look here.' Cee Cee had pulled up a map of the Carmel Valley. She highlighted the areas she was talking about as she mentioned them. 'See this property here? Hotel and spa. See how close it is to the water? That was a no-building zone. Too much erosion. But RedCo — that's the name of the corporation that bought the land, RedCo, get it? — used some pull down at city hall and got a permit anyway. Still, this one environmentalist warned RedCo that any building they put up there would not only be dangerously unstable, but would endanger the seal population that hangs out on the beach below it. Well, check this out.'

Cee Cee's fingers flew over her keyboard. A second later,

a picture of a weird-looking guy with a goatee filled the screen, along with what looked like a newspaper story. 'The environmentalist who was making such a fuss over the seals disappeared four years ago, and no one has seen him since.'

I squinted at the computer screen. It was hard to see in the strong sunlight. 'What do you mean, disappeared?' I asked. 'Like he died?'

'Maybe. Nobody knows. His body was never found if he was killed,' Cee Cee said. 'But check this out.' Her fingers did some quick rat-tat-tatting. 'Another project, this strip mall here, was endangering the habitat of this rare kind of mouse, found only in this area. And this lady here—' Another photo came up on screen. 'She tried to stop it and save the mouse, and poof. She disappeared too.'

'Disappeared,' I echoed. 'Just disappeared?'

'Just disappeared. Problem solved for Mount Beau – that was the name of that project's sponsor. Mount Beau. Beaumont. Get it?'

'We get it,' Adam said. 'But if all these environmentalists connected with Red Beaumont's companies are disappearing, how come nobody has looked into it?'

'Well, for one thing,' Cee Cee said, 'Beaumont Industries made one of the biggest campaign donations in the state to our recently elected governor. They also made considerable contributions to the guy who was voted sheriff.'

'A cover-up?' Adam made a face. 'Come *on*.'

'You're assuming anyone even suspects anything. These people aren't dead, remember. Just gone. Near as I can tell, the attitude seems to be, well, environmentalists are kind of flighty anyway, so who's to say these folks didn't just take off for some bigger, more menacing disaster? All except this one.' Cee Cee hit another button, and a third photo filled the page. 'This lady didn't belong to any kooky save-the-seals group. She owned some land Beaumont Industries had its eye on. They wanted to expand one of their cineplexes. Only she wouldn't sell.'

'Don't tell me,' I said. 'She disappeared.'

'Sure did. And seven years later to the day – seven years being the time after which you can legally declare a missing person dead – Beaumont Industries made an offer to her kids, who jumped on it.'

'Finks,' I said, meaning the lady's kids. I leaned forwards so I could get a better look at her picture.

And had quite a little shock: I was looking at a picture of the ghost who'd been paying me those charming social calls.

OK, well, maybe she didn't look *exactly* the same. But she was white and skinny and had the same haircut. There was certainly enough of a resemblance to make me go, 'That's her!' and point.

Which was, of course, the worst thing I could have done. Because both Cee Cee and Adam turned to look at me.

'That's her who?' Adam wanted to know.

And Cee Cee said, 'Suze, you can't possibly know her. She disappeared over seven years ago, and you just moved here last month.'

I am such a loser.

I couldn't even think of a good excuse, either, I just repeated the one I'd stammered to Tad's father. 'Oh, um, I had this dream and she was in it.'

What was *wrong* with me?

I had not, of course, explained to Cee Cee the reason why I'd wanted her to look up stuff on Red Beaumont, any more than I had told Adam how it was that I knew so much about little Timothy Mahern's cat. I had merely mentioned that Mr Beaumont had said something odd during my brief meeting with him the night before. And that Father Dom had sent me to look for the cat, presumably because Timothy's dad had admitted abandoning it during his weekly confession – only Father Dom, being sworn to secrecy, couldn't actually *tell* me that. I was only, I assured Adam, *surmising . . .*

'A dream?' Adam echoed. 'About some lady who's been dead for seven years? That's weird.'

'It probably wasn't her,' I said quickly, backpedalling for all I was worth. 'In fact, I'm sure it wasn't her. The woman I saw was much . . . taller.' Like I could even tell how tall this woman was by looking at her picture somebody had posted on the Internet.

Adam said, 'You know, Cee Cee has an aunt who dreams about dead people all the time. They visit her, she says.'

I threw Cee Cee a startled glance. Could we, I wondered, be talking about *another* mediator? What, was there some kind of glut of us in the greater peninsula area? I knew Carmel was a popular retirement spot, but this was getting ridiculous.

'She doesn't have dreams about them,' Cee Cee said, and I didn't think I was imagining the level of disgust in her voice. 'Aunt Pru summons the spirits of the dead and she'll tell you what they said. For a small fee.'

'Aunt *Pru?*' I grinned. 'Wow, Cee Cee. I didn't know you had a psychic in the family.'

'She isn't a psychic.' Cee Cee's disgust deepened. 'She's a complete flake. I'm embarrassed to be related to her. Talk to the dead. Right!'

'Don't hold back, Cee Cee,' I said. 'Let us know how you really feel.'

'Well,' Cee Cee said. 'I'm sorry. But—'

'Hey,' Adam interrupted brightly. 'Maybe Aunt Pru could help tell us why –' he bent down for a closer look at the dead woman's photo on Cee Cee's computer screen – 'Mrs Dierdre Fiske here is popping up in Suze's dreams.'

Horrified, I leaned forwards and slammed Cee Cee's laptop closed. 'No thanks,' I said.

Cee Cee, opening her computer back up again, said irritably, 'Nobody fondles the electronics but me, Simon.'

'Aw, come on,' Adam said. 'It'll be fun. Suze's never met Pru. She'll get a big kick out of her. She's a riot.'

Cee Cee muttered, 'Yeah, you know how funny the mentally ill can be.'

I said, hoping to get the subject back on track, 'Um, maybe some other time. Anything else, Cee Cee, that you were able to dig up on Mr Beaumont?'

'You mean other than the fact that he might possibly be killing anyone who stands in the way of his amassing a fortune by raping our forests and beaches?' Cee Cee, who was wearing a khaki rainhat to protect her sensitive skin from the sun, as well as her violet-lensed sunglasses, looked up at me. 'You're not satisfied yet, Simon? Haven't we thoroughly vetted your paramour's closest relations?'

'Yeah,' Adam said. 'It must be reassuring to know that last night you hooked up with a guy who comes from such a nice, stable family, Suze.'

'Hey,' I said with an indignation I was far from actually feeling. 'There's no *proof* Tad's dad is the one who's responsible for those environmentalists' disappearances. And besides, we just had coffee, OK? We did not hook up.'

Cee Cee blinked at me. 'You went out with him, Suze. That's all Adam meant by hooking up.'

'Oh.' Where I come from, hooking up means something else entirely. 'Sorry. I—'

At that moment, Adam let out a shout. 'Spike!'

I whirled around, following his pointing finger. There,

peering out from the dry underbrush, sat the biggest, mean-est-looking cat I'd ever seen. He was the same colour yellow as the grass, which was probably how we'd missed him. He had orange stripes, one chewed-off ear and an extremely nasty look on his face.

'Spike?' I asked softly.

The cat turned his head in my direction and glared at me malevolently.

'Oh, my God,' I said. 'No wonder Tim's dad didn't take him to the animal shelter.'

It took some doing – and the ultimate sacrifice of my Kate Spade book bag, which I'd managed to purchase only at great physical risk at a sample sale back in SoHo – but we finally managed to capture Spike. Once he was zipped up inside my bag, he seemed to resign himself to captivity, although throughout the ride to Safeway, where we went to stock up on litter and food for him, I could hear him work-ing industriously on the bag's lining with his claws. Timothy, I decided, owed me big time.

Especially when Adam, instead of turning up the street to my house, turned in the opposite direction, heading further up the Carmel hills until the big red dome covering the basil-ica of the Mission below us was the size of my thumbnail.

'No,' Cee Cee immediately said as firmly as I've ever heard her say anything. 'Absolutely not. Turn the car around. Turn the car around *now*.'

Only Adam, chuckling diabolically, just sped up.

Holding my Kate Spade bag on my lap, I said, 'Uh, Adam. I don't know where, exactly, you think you're going, but I'd really like to at least get rid of this, um, animal first—'

'Just for a minute,' Adam said. 'The cat'll be all right. Come *on*, Cee. Stop being such a spoilsport.'

Cee Cee was madder than I'd ever seen her. 'I said *no!*' she shouted.

But it was too late. Adam pulled up in front of a little stucco bungalow that had wind chimes hanging all over the place tinkling in the breeze from the bay, and giant hibiscus blossoms turned up towards the late afternoon sun. He put his VW in park and switched off the ignition.

'We'll just pop in to say hi,' he said to Cee Cee. And then he unfastened his seat belt and hopped out of the car.

Cee Cee and I didn't move. She was in the back seat. I was in the front with the cat. From my bag came an ominous rumbling.

'I hesitate to ask,' I said, after a while of sitting there listening to the wind chimes and Spike's steady growling. 'But where are we?'

That question was answered when, a second later, the door to the bungalow burst open and a woman whose hair was the same whitish yellow as Cee Cee's – only so long that she could sit on it – yoo-hooed at us.

'Come in,' Cee Cee's aunt Pru called. 'Please come in! I've been expecting you!'

Cee Cee, not even glancing in her aunt's direction, muttered, 'I just bet you have, you psychic freak.'

Remind me never to tell Cee Cee about the whole mediator thing.

Eleven

'Oh, goodness,' Cee Cee's aunt Pru said. 'There it is again. The ninth key. This is just so strange.'

Cee Cee and I exchanged glances. Strange wasn't quite the word for it.

Not that it was unpleasant. Far from it. At least, in my opinion anyway. Pru Webb, Cee Cee's aunt, was a little odd. That was certainly true.

But her house was very aromatic what with all the scented candles she kept lit everywhere. And she'd been quite the attentive hostess, giving us each a glass of home-made lemonade. It was too bad, of course, that she'd forgotten to put sugar in it, but that kind of forgetfulness apparently wasn't unusual for someone so in touch with the spirit world. Aunt Pru had informed us that her mentor, the most powerful psychic on the West Coast, often couldn't remember his own name because he was channelling so many other souls.

Still, our little visit hadn't been particularly enlightening so far. I had learned, for instance, that according to the lines in my palm, I am going to grow up to have a challenging job in the field of medical research (Yeah! That'll be the day). Cee Cee, meanwhile, is going to be a movie star, and Adam an astronaut.

Seriously. An *astronaut.*

I was, I admit, a little jealous of their future careers, which were clearly a great deal more exciting than my own, but I tried hard to control my envy.

What I'd given up trying to control – and Cee Cee apparently had as well – was Adam. He had told Aunt Pru, before I could stop him, about my 'dream', and now the poor woman was trying – pro bono, mind you – to summon Deirdre Fiske's spirit using tarot cards and a lot of humming.

Only it did not appear to be working because every time she started to turn the cards over, she kept coming up with the same one.

The ninth key.

This was, apparently, upsetting to her. Shaking her head, Aunt Pru – that's what she'd told me to call her – scooped all the cards back into a pile, shuffled them, and then, closing her eyes, pulled one from the middle of the deck, and laid it, face up, for us to see.

Then she opened her eyes, looked down at it and went, 'Again! This doesn't make any sense.'

She wasn't kidding. The idea of anyone summoning a ghost with a deck of cards made no sense whatsoever . . . to me at least. I couldn't even summon them by standing there screaming their names – something I'd tried, believe me – and I'm a mediator. My *job* is to communicate with the undead.

But ghosts aren't dogs. They don't come if you call them. Take my dad for instance. How many times had I wanted – even needed – him? He'd shown up all right: three, four weeks later. Ghosts are way irresponsible for the most part.

But I couldn't exactly explain to Cee Cee's aunt that what she was doing was a huge waste of time . . . and that while she was sitting there doing it, there was a cat trying to eat his way out of my book bag in Adam's car.

Oh, and that a guy who might or might not have been a vampire – but was certainly responsible for the disappearances of quite a number of people – was running around loose. I could only just sit there with this big stupid smile on my face, pretending to be enjoying myself, while really I was itching to get home and on the phone with Father D, so we could figure out what we were going to do about Red Beaumont.

'Oh, dear,' Aunt Pru said. She was very pretty, Cee Cee's aunt Pru. An albino like her niece, her eyes were the colour of violets. She wore a flowing sundress of the same shade. The contrast her long white hair made against the purple of her dress was startling – and cool. Cee Cee, I knew, was probably going to look just like her aunt Pru someday, once she got rid of the braces and puppy fat, that is.

Which was probably why Cee Cee couldn't stand her.

'What can this mean?' Aunt Pru muttered to herself. 'The hermit. The hermit.'

There appeared, from what I could see, to be a hermit on the card Aunt Pru kept turning over and over. Not of the crab variety either, but the old-man-living-in-a-cave type. I didn't know what a hermit had to do with Mrs Fiske either, but one thing I did know: I was bored stupid.

'One more time,' Aunt Pru said, sending a cautious glance in Cee Cee's direction. Cee Cee had made it clear that we didn't have all day. I was the one who needed to get home most, of course. I had an Ackerman dinner to contend with. Kung pao chicken night. If I was late, my mom was going to kill me.

'Um,' I said. 'Ms Webb?'

'Aunt Pru, darling,'

'Right. Aunt Pru. May I use your phone?'

'Of course.' Aunt Pru didn't even glance at me. She was too busy channelling.

I wandered out of the darkened room and went out into the hallway. There was an old-fashioned rotary phone on a little table there. I dialled my own number – after a brief struggle to remember it since I'd only had it for a few weeks – and when Dopey picked up, I asked him to tell my mother that I hadn't forgotten about dinner and was on my way home.

Dopey not very graciously informed me that he was on the other line and that because he was not my social secretary, and had no intention of taking any messages for me, I should call back later.

'Who are you talking to?' I asked. 'Debbie, your love slave?'

Dopey responded by hanging up on me. Some people have no sense of humour.

I put down the receiver and was standing there looking at this zodiac calendar and wondering if I was in some kind of celestial good-luck zone – considering what had happened with Tad and all – when someone standing right beside me said, in an irritated voice, 'Well? What do you want?'

I jumped nearly a foot. I swear, I've been doing this all my life, but I just can't get used to it. I would so rather have some other secret power – like the ability to do long division in my head – than this mediator crap, I swear.

I spun around, and there she was, standing in Aunt Pru's entranceway, looking cranky in a gardening hat and gloves.

She was not the same woman who'd been waking me up at night. They were similar body types, little and slender, with the same pixyish haircut, but this woman was easily in her sixties.

'Well?' She eyed me. 'I don't have all day. What did you call me for?'

I stared at the woman in wonder. The truth was, I hadn't

98

called her. I hadn't done anything, except stand there and wonder if Tad was still going to like me when Mercury retrograded into Aquarius.

'Mrs Fiske?' I whispered.

'Yes, that's me.' The old lady looked me up and down. 'You *are* the one who called me, aren't you?'

'Um.' I glanced back towards the room where I could still hear Aunt Pru saying, apparently to herself, since neither Cee Cee nor Adam could have understood what she was talking about, 'But the ninth key has no *bearing* . . .'

I turned back to Mrs Fiske. 'I guess so,' I said.

Mrs Fiske looked me up and down. It was clear she didn't much like what she was seeing. 'Well?' she said. 'What is it?'

Where to begin? Here was a woman who'd disappeared, and been presumed dead, for almost half as long as I'd been alive. I glanced back at Aunt Pru and the others, just to make sure they weren't looking in my direction, and then whispered, 'I just need to know, Mrs Fiske . . . Mr Beaumont. He killed you, didn't he?'

Mrs Fiske suddenly stopped looking so crabby. Her eyes, which were very blue, fixed on mine. She said, in a shocked voice, 'My God. My God, finally . . . someone knows. Someone finally knows.'

I reached out to lay a reassuring hand upon her arm. 'Yes, Mrs Fiske,' I said. 'I know. And I'm going to stop him from hurting anybody else.'

Mrs Fiske shrugged my hand off and blinked at me. '*You?*' She still looked stunned, but now in a different way.

I realized how when she burst out laughing.

'*You're* going to stop him?' she cackled. 'You're . . . you're a baby!'

'I'm no baby,' I assured her. 'I'm a mediator.'

'A mediator?' To my surprise, Mrs Fiske threw back her

head and laughed harder. 'A mediator. Oh, well, that makes it all better, doesn't it?'

I wanted to tell her I didn't really care for her tone, but Mrs Fiske didn't give me a chance.

'And you think you can stop Beaumont?' she demanded. 'Honey, you've got a lot to learn.'

I didn't think this was very polite. I said, 'Look, lady, I may be young, but I know what I'm doing. Now, just tell me where he hid your body, and—'

'Are you insane?' Mrs Fiske finally stopped laughing. Now she shook her head. 'There's nothing left of me. Beaumont's no amateur, you know. He made sure there weren't any mistakes. And there weren't. You won't find a scrap of evidence to implicate him. Believe me. The guy's a monster. A real bloodsucker.' Then her mouth hardened. 'Though no worse, I suppose, than my own kids. Selling my land to that leech! Listen, you. You're a mediator. Give my kids this message for me: tell them I hope they burn in—'

'Hey, Suze.' Cee Cee suddenly appeared in the hallway. 'The witch has given up. She has to consult her guru, 'cause she keeps coming up bust.'

I threw a frantic look at Mrs Fiske. Wait! I still hadn't had a chance to ask her how she'd died! Was Red Beaumont really a vampire? Had he sucked all the life out of her? Did she mean he was *literally* a bloodsucking leech?

But it was too late. Cee Cee, still coming towards me, walked right through what looked – and felt – to me like a little old lady in a gardening hat and gloves. And the little old lady shimmered indignantly.

Don't, I wanted to scream. Don't go!

'Ew,' Cee Cee said with a little shudder as she threw off the last of Mrs Fiske's clinging aura. 'Come on. Let's get out of here. This place gives me the creeps.'

I never did find out what Mrs Fiske's message to her kids was – though I had a bit of an idea. The old lady, with a last, disgusted look at me, disappeared.

Just as Aunt Pru came into the hallway, looking apologetic.

'I'm so sorry, Suzie,' she said. 'I really tried, but the Santa Anas have been particularly strong this year, and so there's been a lot of interference in the spiritual pathways I normally utilize.'

Maybe that explained how I had managed to summon the spirit of Mrs Fiske. Could I do it again, I wondered, and this time remember to ask exactly how Red Beaumont had killed her?

Adam, as we headed back towards his car, looked immensely pleased with himself.

'Well, Suze?' he said, as he held open the passenger side door for Cee Cee and me. 'You ever in your life met anybody like that?'

I had, of course. Being a magnet for the souls of the unhappily dead, I'd met people from all walks of life, including an Incan priestess, several witch doctors, and even a Pilgrim who'd been burned at the stake as a witch.

But since it seemed so important to him, I smiled and said, 'Not exactly,' which was the truth, in a way.

Cee Cee didn't look too thrilled with the fact that one of her family members had managed to provide the boy she – let's face it – had a huge crush on with so much entertainment. She crawled into the back seat and glowered there. Cee Cee was a straight-A student who didn't believe in anything that couldn't be proved scientifically, especially anything to do with the hereafter . . . which made the fact that her parents had stuck her in Catholic school a bit problematic.

More problematic to me, however, than Cee Cee's lack of faith or my newfound ability to summon spirits at will was

101

what I was going to do with this cat. While we'd been inside Aunt Pru's house, he'd managed to chew a hole through one corner of my bag, and now he kept poking one paw through it, swiping blindly with claws fully outstretched at whatever came his way – primarily me, since I was the one holding the bag. Adam, no matter how hard I wheedled, wouldn't take the cat home with him, and Cee Cee just laughed when I asked her. I knew there was no way I was going to talk Father Dominic into taking Spike to live in the rectory: Sister Ernestine would never allow it.

Which left me only one alternative. And I really, really wasn't happy about it. Besides what the cat had done to the inside of my bag – God only knew what he'd do to my room – there was the fact that I was pretty sure felines were ver-boten in the Ackerman household due to Dopey's delicate sensitivity to their dander.

So I still had the stupid cat, plus a Safeway bag containing a litter box, the litter itself, and about twenty cans of Fancy Feast, when Adam pulled up to my house to drop me off.

'Hey,' he said appreciatively, as I struggled to get out of the car. 'Who's visiting you guys? The Pope?'

I looked where he was pointing . . . and then my jaw dropped.

Parked in our driveway was a big, black stretch limo, just like the kind I'd fantasized about going to the prom with Tad in!

'Uh,' I said, slamming the door to Adam's VW shut. 'I'll see you guys.'

I hurried up the driveway, with Spike, determined not to be forgotten just because he'd been zipped into a book bag, growling and spitting the whole way. As I was coming up the front steps to the porch, I heard the rumble of voices com-ing from the living room.

And when I stepped through the front door, and I saw who those voices belonged to . . . well, Spike came pretty close to becoming a kitty pancake, I squeezed that bag so tight to my chest.

Because sitting there chatting amiably with my mother and holding a cup of tea was none other than Thaddeus 'Red' Beaumont.

Twelve

'Oh, Suzie,' my mom said, turning around as I came into the house. 'Hello, honey. Look who stopped by to see you. Mr Beaumont and his son.'

It was only then that I noticed Tad was there too. He was standing by the wall that had all of our family photos on it – which weren't many since we'd only been a family for a few weeks. Mostly they were just school photos of me and my stepbrothers, and pictures from Andy and my mom's wedding.

Tad grinned at me, then pointed at a photo of me at the age of ten – in which I was missing both my front teeth – and said, 'Nice smile.'

I managed to give him a reasonable facsimile of that smile, minus the missing teeth. 'Hi,' I said.

'Tad and Mr Beaumont were on their way home,' my mom said, 'and they thought they'd stop by and see if you'd have dinner with them tonight. I told them I didn't think you had any other plans. You don't, do you, Suze?'

My mom, I could tell, was practically frothing at the mouth at the idea of me having dinner with this guy and his kid. My mom would have frothed at the mouth at the idea of me having dinner with Darth Vader and his kid, that's how hot she was to get me a boyfriend. All my mom has ever wanted is for me to be a normal teenage girl.

But if she thought Red Beaumont was prime in-law material, boy, was she barking up the wrong tree.

And speaking of barking, I had suddenly become an object of considerable interest to Max, who had started sniffing around my book bag and whining.

'Um,' I said. 'Would you mind if I just ran upstairs and, um, dumped my stuff off?'

'Not at all,' Mr Beaumont said. 'Not at all. Take your time. I was just telling your mother about your article. The one you're doing for the school paper.'

'Yes, Suzie,' my mom said, turning around in her seat with this huge smile. 'You never told me you were working for the school paper. How exciting!'

I looked at Mr Beaumont. He smiled blandly back at me.

And suddenly, I had a very bad feeling.

Oh, not that Mr Beaumont was going to get up, come over, and bite me on the neck. Not that.

But all of a sudden, I got this very bad feeling that he was going to tell my mother the real reason I'd gone to visit him the night before. Not the newspaper article thing, but the thing about my dream.

Which my mom would instantly suspect was you-know-what. If she heard I'd been going around feeding wealthy real estate tycoons lines about psychic dreams, I'd be grounded from here until graduation.

And the worst part of it was, considering how much trouble I used to be in all the time back in New York, I wasn't at all eager to let my mom in on the fact that I was actually up to even *more* stuff on *this* side of the country. I mean, she really had no clue. She thought all of it – the fact that I'd constantly missed my curfew, my run-ins with the police, my suspensions, the bad grades – were behind us, over, kaput, the end. We were on a new coast, making a new start.

And my mom was just so *happy* about it.

So I said, 'Oh, yeah, the *article* I'm doing,' and gave Mr Beaumont a meaningful look. At least, I hoped it would be meaningful. And I hoped what it meant to him was: don't spill the beans, buster, or you'll pay for it big time.

Though I'm not certain how scared a guy like Red Beaumont would actually be of a sixteen-year-old girl.

He wasn't. He sent a look right back at me. A look that said, if I wasn't mistaken: I won't spill the beans, sister, if you play along like a good little girl.

I nodded to let him know I'd gotten the message, whirled around, and hurried up the stairs.

Well, I figured as I went, Max loping at my heels, still trying to get a gander into my bag, at least Tad was with him. Mr Beaumont certainly wasn't going to be able to bite me on the neck with his own kid in the room. Tad, I was pretty sure, wasn't a vampire. And he didn't seem like the kind of guy who'd just stand by and let his dad kill his date.

And with any luck, that guy Marcus would be there. Marcus certainly wouldn't allow his employer to sink his fangs in me.

I wasn't too surprised when, as we reached the door to my bedroom, Max suddenly turned tail and, with a yelp, ran in the opposite direction. He wasn't too thrilled by Jesse's presence.

Neither, I figured, was Spike going to be. But Spike didn't have any other choice.

I went into my room and took the litter box out of my giant Safeway bag and shoved it under the sink in my bathroom, then filled it with litter. In the centre of my room where I'd left my book bag came some pretty unearthly howling. That paw kept shooting out of the hole Spike had chewed, and feeling around for something to claw.

'I'm going as fast as I can,' I grumbled as I poured some water into a bowl then opened a can of food and left it on a plate on the floor along with the water.

Then, making sure I unzipped it away from me, I opened the bag.

Spike came tearing out like . . . well, more like the Tasmanian Devil than any cat I'd ever seen. He was completely out of control. He tore around the room three times before he spotted the food, skidded suddenly to a halt, and began to suck it down.

'What,' I heard Jesse say, 'is *that*?'

I looked up. I hadn't seen Jesse since our fight the night before. He was leaning against one of my bed-posts – my mom had gone whole hog when she'd decorated my room, going for the frilly dressing table, canopy bed, the works – looking down at the cat like it was some kind of alien life form.

'It's a cat,' I said. 'I didn't have any choice. It's just until I find a home for it.'

Jesse eyed Spike dubiously. 'Are you sure it's a cat? It doesn't look like any cat I've ever seen. It looks more like . . . what do they call them? Those small horses. Oh yes, a pony.'

'I'm sure it's a cat,' I said. 'Listen, Jesse, I'm kind of in a jam here.'

He nodded at Spike. 'I can see that.'

'Not about the cat,' I said, quickly. 'It's about Tad.'

Jesse's expression, which had been a fairly pleasant, teasing one, suddenly darkened. If I hadn't been sure he didn't give a hang about me aside from as a friend, I'd have sworn he was jealous.

'He's downstairs,' I said quickly, before Jesse could start yelling at me again for being too easy on a first date. 'With his father. They want me to come over for dinner. And I'm not going to be able to get out of it.'

Jesse muttered some stuff in Spanish. Judging from the look on his face, whatever he said hadn't exactly been an expression of regret that he, too, had not been invited.

'The thing is,' I went on, 'I've found out some things about Mr Beaumont, things that kind of make me . . . well, nervous. So could you, um, do me a favour?'

Jesse straightened. He seemed pretty surprised. I don't really ask him to do me favours all that often.

'Of course, *querida*,' he said, and my heart gave a little flip-flop inside my chest at the caressing tone he always gave that word. I didn't even know what it meant.

Why am I so *pathetic*?

'Look,' I said, my voice squeakier than ever, unfortunately, 'if I'm not back by midnight, can you just let Father Dominic know that he should probably call the police?'

As I'd been speaking, I'd taken out a new bag, a Kate Spade knock-off, and I was slipping the stuff I normally use for ghost-busting into it. You know, my flashlight, pliers, gloves, the roll of dimes I keep in my fist ever since my mom found and confiscated my brass knuckles, pepper spray, bowie knife, and, oh, yeah, a pencil. It was the best I could come up with in lieu of a wooden stake. I don't believe in vampires, but I do believe in being prepared.

'You want *me* to speak to the priest?'

Jesse sounded shocked. I guess I couldn't blame him. While I'd never exactly forbidden him from speaking to Father Dom, I'd never actually encouraged him either. I certainly hadn't told him why I was so reluctant for the two of them to meet – Father D was sure to have an embolism over the living arrangements – but I hadn't exactly given him the all clear to go strolling into Father Dominic's office.

'Yes,' I said. 'I do.'

Jesse looked confused. 'But, Susannah,' he said. 'If he's this dangerous, this man, why are you—'

Someone tapped on my bedroom door. 'Suzie?' my mom called. 'You decent?'

I grabbed my bag. 'Yeah, Mom,' I said. I threw Jesse one last, pleading look, and then I hurried from the room, careful not to let out Spike, who'd finished his meal and was doing some pretty serious nosing around for more food.

In the hallway, my mother looked at me curiously. 'Is everything all right, Suzie?' she asked me. 'You were up here for so long . . .'

'Uh, yeah,' I said. 'Listen, Mom—'

'Suzie, I didn't know things were so serious with this boy.' My mom took my arm and started steering me back down the stairs. 'He's so handsome! And so sweet! It's just so adorable, his wanting you to have dinner with him and his father.'

I wondered how sweet she'd have thought it if she'd known about Mrs Fiske. My mom had been a television news journalist for over twenty years. She'd won a couple of national awards for some of her investigations, and when she'd first started looking for a job on the West Coast, she'd pretty much had her pick of news stations.

And a sixteen-year-old albino with a laptop and a modem knew a heck of a lot more about Red Beaumont than she did.

It just goes to show that people only know what they want to.

'Yeah,' I said. 'About Mr Beaumont, Mom. I don't think I really—'

'And what's all this about you writing a story for the school paper? Suze, I didn't know you were interested in journalism.'

My mom looked almost as happy as she had the day she and Andy had finally tied the knot. And considering that that was about as happy as I'd ever seen her – since my dad had died anyway – that was pretty happy.

'Suzie, I'm just so proud of you,' she gushed. 'You really are finding yourself out here. You know how I used to worry, back in New York. You always seemed to be getting into trouble. But it looks as if things are really turning around . . . for the both of us.'

This was when I should have said, 'Listen, Mom. About Red Beaumont? OK, definitely up to no good, possibly a *vampire*. Enough said. Now could you tell him I've got a migraine and that I can't go to dinner?'

But I didn't. I couldn't. I just kept remembering that look Mr Beaumont had given me. He was going to tell my mother. He was going to tell my mother the truth. About how I'd busted into his place under false pretences, about that dream I'd said I'd had.

About how I can talk to the dead.

No. No, that was not going to happen. I had finally gotten to a point in my life where my mom was beginning to be proud of me, to trust me, even. It was kind of like New York had been this really bad nightmare from which she and I had finally woken up. Here in California I was popular. I was normal. I was cool. I was the kind of daughter my mom had always wanted instead of the social reject who'd constantly been dragged home by the police for trespassing and creating a public nuisance. I was no longer forced to lie to a therapist twice a week. I wasn't serving permanent detention. I didn't have to listen to my mother cry into her pillow at night, or notice her surreptitiously starting a Valium regimen whenever parent-teacher conferences rolled around.

Hey, with the exception of the poison oak, even my skin had cleared up. I was a completely different kid.

I took a deep breath.

'Sure, Mom,' I said. 'Sure, things are really turning around for us.'

Thirteen

He didn't eat.

He'd invited me to dinner, but he didn't eat.

Tad did. Tad ate a lot.

Well, boys always do. I mean, look at mealtime in the Ackerman household. It was like something out of a Jack London novel. Only instead of White Fang and the rest of the sled dogs, you have Sleepy, Dopey and even Doc, chowing down like it might be their last meal.

At least Tad had good manners. He'd held my chair for me as I'd sat down. He actually employed a napkin, instead of simply wiping his hands on his pants, one of Dopey's favourite tricks. And he made sure I was served first, so there was plenty to go around.

Especially since his father wasn't eating.

But he did sit with us. He sat at the head of the table with a glass of red wine – at least, it *looked* like wine – and beamed at me as each course was presented. You read that right: courses. I'd never had a meal with courses before. I mean, Andy was a good cook and all, but he usually served everything all at once – you know, entrée, salad, rolls, the whole thing at the same time.

At Red Beaumont's house, the courses all came individually, served by waiters with this big flourish; two waiters, so that each of our plates – Tad's and mine, I mean – were put down at the same time, and nobody's food got cold while he or she was waiting for everyone else to be served.

The first course was a consommé, which turned out to have bits of lobster floating in it. That was pretty good. Then came some kind of fancy sea scallops in this tangy green sauce. Then came lamb with garlic mashed potatoes, then salad, a mess of weeds with balsamic vinegar all over them, followed by a tray on which there were all these different kinds of stinky cheeses.

And Mr Beaumont didn't touch a thing. He said he was on a special diet and had already had his dinner.

And even though I don't believe in vampires, I just kept sitting there wondering what his special diet consisted of, and if Mrs Fiske and those missing environmentalists had provided any part of it.

I know. I *know*. But I couldn't help it. It was creeping me out the way he just sat there drinking his wine and smiling as Tad chatted about basketball. From what I could gather – I was having trouble concentrating, what with wondering why Father D hadn't given me a bottle of holy water when he'd first realized there might be a chance we were dealing with a vampire – Tad was Robert Louis Stevenson's star player.

As I sat there listening to Tad go on about all the three-pointers he'd scored, I realized with a sinking heart that not only was he possibly the descendant of a vampire, but also that, except for kissing, he and I really had no mutual interests. I mean, I don't have a whole lot of time for hobbies, what with homework and the mediating stuff, but I was pretty sure if I'd had an interest, it wouldn't be chasing a ball up and down a wooden court.

But maybe kissing was enough. Maybe kissing was the

113

only thing that mattered anyway. Maybe kissing could overcome the whole vampire/basketball thing.

Because as we got up from the table to go to the living room, where dessert, I was told, would be served, Tad picked up my hand – which was, by the way, still a bit poison oaky, but he evidently didn't care; there was still a healthy amount of it on the back of his neck, after all – and gave it a squeeze.

And all of a sudden I was convinced that I had probably way overreacted back home when I'd asked Jesse to have Father Dominic call the cops if I wasn't home by midnight. I mean, yeah, there were people who might think Red Beaumont was a vampire, and he certainly may have made his fortune in a creepy way.

But that didn't necessarily make him a bad guy. And we didn't have any actual *proof* he really had killed all those people. And what about that dead woman who kept showing up in my bedroom? She was convinced Red *hadn't* killed her. She'd gone to great lengths to assure me that he was innocent of her death, at least. Maybe Mr Beaumont wasn't that bad.

'I thought you were mad at me,' Tad whispered as we followed Yoshi, who was carrying a tray of coffee – herbal tea for me – into the living room ahead of us.

'Why should I be mad at you?' I asked curiously.

'Well, last night,' Tad whispered, 'when I was kissing you—'

All at once I remembered how I'd seen Jesse sitting there, and how I'd screamed bloody murder over it. Blushing, I said, unable to look Tad in the eye, 'Oh, that. That was just . . . I thought . . . I saw a spider.'

'A spider?' Tad pulled me down on to this black leather couch next to him. In front of the couch there was a big

114

coffee table that looked like it was made out of Plexiglas. 'In my *car*?'

'I've got a thing about spiders,' I said.

'Oh.' Tad looked at me with his sleepy brown eyes. 'I thought maybe you thought I was – well, a little forward. Kissing you like that, I mean.'

'Oh, no,' I said with a laugh that I hoped sounded all sophisticated, as if guys were going around sticking their tongues in my mouth all the time.

'Good,' Tad said, and he put his arm around my neck and started pulling me towards him—

But then his dad walked in, and went, 'Now, where we were? Oh, yes. Susannah, you were going to tell us all about how your class is trying to raise money to restore the statue of Father Serra that was so unfortunately vandalized last week . . .'

Tad and I pulled quickly apart.

'Uh, sure,' I said. And I started telling the long, boring tale, which actually involved a bake sale, of all things. As I was telling it, Tad reached over to the massive glass coffee table in front of him and picked up a cup of coffee. He put cream and sugar into it, then took a sip.

'And then,' I said, really convinced now that the whole thing had been a giant misunderstanding – the thing about Tad's dad, I mean – 'we found out it's actually cheaper to get a whole new statue cast than to repair the old one, but then it wouldn't be an authentic . . . well, whoever the artist is, I forget. So we're still trying to figure it out. If we repair the old one, there'll be a seam that will show where the neck was reattached, but we could hide the seam if we raise the collar of Father Serra's cassock. So there's some wrangling going on about the historical accuracy of a high-collared cassock, and—'

It was at this point in my narration that Tad suddenly pitched forwards and plowed face-first into my lap.

I blinked down at him. Was I really *that* boring? God, no wonder no one had ever asked me out before.

Then I realized Tad wasn't asleep at all. He was *unconscious*.

I looked over at Mr Beaumont, who was gazing sadly at his son from the leather couch opposite mine.

'Oh, my God,' I said.

Mr Beaumont sighed. 'Fast-acting, isn't it?' he said.

Horrified, I exclaimed, 'God, poison your kid, why don't you?'

'He hasn't been poisoned,' Mr Beaumont said, looking appalled. 'Do you think I would do something like that to my own boy? He's merely drugged, of course. In a few hours he'll wake up and not remember a thing. He'll just feel extremely well rested.'

I was struggling to push Tad off me. The guy wasn't huge or anything, but he was dead weight, and it was no easy task getting his face out of my lap.

'Listen,' I said to Mr Beaumont as I struggled to squirm out from under his son, 'you better not try anything.'

With one hand I pushed Tad, while with the other I surreptitiously unzipped my bag. I hadn't let it out of my sight since I'd entered the house, in spite of the fact that Yoshi had tried to take it and put it with my coat. A few squirts of pepper spray, I decided, would suit Mr Beaumont very nicely in the event that he tried anything physical.

'I mean it,' I assured him, as I slipped a hand inside my bag and fumbled around inside it for the pepper spray. 'It would be a really bad idea for you to mess with me, Mr Beaumont. I'm not who you think I am.'

Mr Beaumont just looked more sad when he heard that. He said, with another big sigh, 'Neither am I.'

'No,' I said. I had found the pepper spray, and now, one-handed, I worked the little plastic safety cap off it. 'You think I'm just some stupid girl your son's brought home for dinner. But I'm not.'

'Of course you're not,' Mr Beaumont said. 'That's why it was so important that I speak with you again. You talk to the dead, and I, you see . . .'

I eyed him suspiciously. 'You what?'

'Well.' He looked embarrassed. 'I make them that way.'

What had that dopey lady in my bedroom meant when she insisted he hadn't tried to kill her? Of course he had! Just like he'd killed Mrs Fiske!

Just like he was getting ready to kill me.

'Don't think I don't appreciate your sense of humour, Mr Beaumont,' I said. 'Because I do. I really do. I think you're a very funny guy. So I hope you won't take this personally—'

And I sprayed him, full in the face.

Or at least I meant to. I held the nozzle in his direction and I pressed down on it. Only all that came out was sort of *spliff* noise.

No paralyzing pepper spray though. None at all.

And then I remembered that bottle of Paul Mitchell styling spritz that had leaked all over the bottom of my bag the last time I was at the beach. That stuff, mixed with sand, had gunked up nearly everything I owned. And now, it seemed, it had coated the hole my pepper spray was supposed to squirt out of.

'Oh,' Mr Beaumont said. He looked very disappointed in me. 'Mace? Now is that fair, Susannah?'

I knew what I had to do. I threw down the useless bottle and started to make a run for it—

117

Too late, however. He lashed out – so suddenly, I didn't even have time to move – and seized my wrist in a grip that, let me tell you, hurt quite a bit.

'You better let go of me,' I advised him. 'I mean it. You'll regret it—'

But he ignored me, and spoke without the least bit of animosity, almost as if I hadn't just tried to paralyze his mucus membranes.

'I'm sorry if I seemed flippant before,' he said, apologetically. 'But I really mean it. I have, unfortunately, made some very serious errors in judgement that have resulted in several persons losing their lives and at my own hands . . . It is imperative that you help me speak to them, to assure them that I am very, very sorry for what I've done.'

I blinked at him. 'OK,' I said. 'That's it. I'm out of here.'

But no matter how hard I pulled on my arm, I couldn't break free of his vicelike grip. The guy was surprisingly strong for someone's dad.

'I know that to you I seem horrible,' he went on. 'A monster, even. But I'm not. I'm really not.'

'Tell that to Mrs Fiske,' I grunted as I tugged on my arm.

Mr Beaumont didn't seem to have heard me. 'You can't imagine what it's like. The hours I've spent torturing myself over what I've done . . .'

With my free hand, I was rooting through my bag again. 'Well, a real good prescriptive for guilt, I've always found, is confessing.' My fingers closed over the roll of dimes. No. No good. He had my best punching arm. 'Why don't you let me make a phone call, and we can get the police over here, and you can tell them all about it. How does that sound?'

'No,' Mr Beaumont said solemnly. 'That's no good. I highly doubt the police would have any respect whatsoever for my somewhat, well, *special* needs . . .'

And then Mr Beaumont did something totally unexpect-ed. He smiled at me. Ruefully, but still, a smile.

He had smiled at me before, of course, but I had always been across the room, or at least the width of a coffee table away. Now I was right there, right in his face.

And when he smiled, I was given a very special glimpse of something I certainly never expected to see in my lifetime:

The pointiest incisors ever.

OK, I'll admit it. I freaked. I may have been battling ghosts all of my life, but that didn't mean I was at all pre-pared for my first encounter with a real live vampire. I mean, ghosts, I knew from experience, were real.

But vampires? Vampires were the stuff of nightmares, mythological creatures like Bigfoot and the Loch Ness monster. I mean, come on.

But here, right in front of me, smiling this completely sick-ening my-kid-is-an-honour-student kind of smile at me, was an actual real-life vampire in the flesh.

Now I knew why, when Marcus had shown up that day in Mr Beaumont's office, he'd kept looking at my neck. He'd been checking to make sure his boss hadn't tried to go for my jugular.

I guess that's why, considering that my free hand was still inside my shoulder bag, I did what I did next.

Which was grasp the pencil I'd put in there at the last minute, pull it out, and plunge it, with all my might, into the centre of Mr Beaumont's sweater.

For a second, both of us froze. Both Mr Beaumont and I stared at the pencil sticking out of his chest.

Then Mr Beaumont said, in a very surprised voice, 'Oh, my.'

To which I replied, 'Eat lead.'

And then he pitched forwards, missing the glass coffee

table by only a few inches, and ended up on the floor between the couch and the fireplace.

Where he lay unmoving for several long moments, during which all I could do was massage the wrist he'd been clutching so hard.

He didn't, I noticed after a while, crumble into dust the way vampires on TV did. Nor did he burst into flame as vampires in the movies often do. Instead, he just lay there.

And then, little by little, the reality of what I had just done sank in:

I had just killed my boyfriend's dad.

Fourteen

Well, OK, Tad wasn't exactly my boyfriend, and I had honestly believed that his dad was a vampire.

But guess what? He wasn't. And I had killed him.

How unpopular was *that* going to make me?

And this little bubble of hysteria started rising up into my throat. I could tell I was going to scream. I really didn't want to. But there I was in a room with an unconscious kid and his psycho dad, whom I had just staked through the heart with a Number Two pencil. How could I help thinking, You know, they are so totally going to kick me off the student council . . .

Come on. You'd have started screaming too.

But no sooner had I sucked in a lungful of air and was getting ready to let it out in a shriek guaranteed to bring Yoshi and all those waiters who'd served me dinner come running, than someone standing behind me asked sharply, 'What happened here?'

I spun around. And there, looking stunned, stood Marcus, Red Beaumont's secretary.

I said the first thing that came into my head, which was, 'I didn't mean to, I swear it. Only he was scaring me, so I stabbed him.'

Marcus, dressed much like the last time I'd seen him, in a

suit and tie, rushed towards me. Not towards his boss, who was sprawled out on the floor. But towards me.

'Are you all right?' he demanded, grabbing me by the shoulders and looking all up and down my body . . . but mostly at my neck. 'Did he hurt you?'

Marcus's face was white with anxiety.

'*I'm* fine,' I said. I was starting to feel a lump in my throat. 'It's your boss you ought to be worried about . . .' My gaze flitted toward Tad, still face-down on the couch. 'Oh, and his kid. He poisoned his kid.'

Marcus went over to Tad and pried open one of his eyelids. Then he bent and listened to his breathing. 'No,' he said, almost to himself. 'Not poisoned. Just drugged.'

'Oh,' I said with a nervous laugh. 'Oh, then that's OK.'

What the hell was going on here? Was this guy for real?

He seemed so. He was obviously very concerned. He shoved the coffee table out of the way, then bent and turned his boss over.

I had to look away. I didn't think I could bear to see that pencil sticking out of Mr Beaumont's chest. I mean, I had rammed ghosts in the chest with all sorts of stuff – pickaxes, butcher's knives, tent poles, whatever was handy. But the thing about ghosts is . . . well, they're already dead. Tad's father had been alive when I'd jabbed that pencil into him.

Oh, God, *why* had I let Father Dom put that stupid vampire idea into my head? What kind of idiot believes in vampires? I must have been out of my mind.

'Is he . . .' I could barely choke the question out. I had to keep my gaze on Tad because if I looked down at his dad, I had a feeling I'd hurl all that lamb and mesclun salad. Even in my anxiety I couldn't help noticing that, unconscious, Tad still looked pretty hot. He certainly wasn't drooling or anything. 'Is he dead?'

And I thought my mother was going to be mad if she found out about the mediator thing. Could you imagine how mad she'd be if she found out I'm a teenage killer?

Marcus's voice sounded surprised. 'Of couse he's not dead,' he said. 'Just fainted. You must have given him quite a little scare.'

I snuck a peek in his direction. He had straightened up, and was standing there with my pencil in his hands. I looked hastily away, my stomach lurching.

'Is this what you used on him?' Marcus asked in a wry voice. When I nodded silently, still not willing to glance in his direction in case I caught a glimpse of Mr Beaumont's blood, he said, 'Don't worry. It didn't go in very far. You hit his sternum.'

Jeesh. Good thing Red Beaumont hadn't turned out to be the real thing or I'd have been in serious trouble. I couldn't even stake a guy properly. I really must be losing my touch.

As it was, all I had succeeded in doing was making a complete ass of myself. I said, still feeling that little bubble of hysteria in my chest, which I blamed for causing me to babble a little incoherently, 'He poisoned Tad, and then he grabbed me, and I just freaked out . . .'

Marcus left his boss's unconscious body and laid a comforting hand on my arm. He said, 'Shhh, I know, I know,' in a soothing voice.

'I'm really sorry,' I jabbered on. 'But he has that thing about sunlight, and then he wouldn't eat, and then when he smiled, he had those pointy teeth, and I really thought—'

'—he was a vampire.' Marcus, to my surprise, finished my sentence for me. 'I know, Miss Simon.'

I'm embarrassed to admit it, but the truth is, I was pretty close to bursting into tears. Marcus's admission, however, made me forget all about my urge to break down into big weepy sobs.

'You *know*?' I echoed, staring up at him incredulously.

He nodded. His expression was grim. 'It's what his doctors call a fixation. He's on medication for it, and most days, he does all right. But sometimes, when we aren't careful, he skips a dose, and . . . well, you can see the results for yourself. He becomes convinced that he is a dangerous vampire who has killed dozens of people—'

'Yeah,' I said. 'He mentioned that too.' And had looked very upset about it too.

'But I assure you, Miss Simon, that he isn't in any way a menace to society. He's actually quite harmless – he's never hurt a soul.'

My gaze strayed over towards Tad. Marcus must have noticed because he added quickly, 'Well, let's just say he's never caused any *permanent* damage.'

Permanent damage? Your own dad slipping you a mickey wasn't considered permanent damage around here? And how did that explain Mrs Fiske and those missing environmentalists?

'I can't apologize enough to you, Miss Simon,' Marcus was saying. He had put his arm around me, and was walking me away from the couch, and towards, of all things, the front entranceway. 'I'm very sorry you had to witness this disturbing scene.'

I glanced over my shoulder. Behind me, Yoshi had appeared. He turned Tad over so his face wasn't squashed into the seat cushion, then draped a blanket over him while a couple of other guys hauled Mr Beaumont to his feet. He murmured something and rolled his head around.

Not dead. Definitely not dead.

'Of course, I needn't point out to you that none of this

124

would have happened –' Marcus didn't sound quite so apologetic as he had before – 'if you hadn't played that little prank on him last night. Mr Beaumont is not a well man. He is very easily agitated. And one thing that gets him particularly excited is any mention whatsoever of the occult. The so-called dream that you described to him only served to trigger another one of his episodes.'

I felt that I had to try, at least, to defend myself. And so I said, 'Well, how was I supposed to know that? I mean, if he's so prone to episodes, why don't you keep him locked up?'

'Because this isn't the Middle Ages, young lady.'

Marcus removed his arm from around my shoulders and stood looking down at me very severely.

'Today, physicians prefer to treat persons suffering from disorders like the one Mr Beaumont has with medication and therapy rather than keeping him in isolation from his family,' Marcus informed me. 'Tad's father can function normally, and even well, so long as little girls who don't know what's good for them keep their noses out of his business.'

Ouch! That was harsh. I had to remind myself that I wasn't the bad guy here. I mean, *I* wasn't the one running around insisting I was a vampire.

And I hadn't caused a bunch of people to disappear just because they'd stood in the way of my building another strip mall.

But even as I thought it, I wondered if it were true. I mean, it didn't seem as if Tad's father had enough marbles rolling around in his head to organize something as sophisticated as a kidnapping and murder. Either my weirdo meter was out of whack or there was something seriously wrong here . . . and a mere 'fixation' just didn't explain it. What, I wondered, about Mrs Fiske? She was dead and Mr Beaumont had killed her – she'd said so herself. Marcus was obviously trying to downplay the severity of his employer's psychosis.

Or was he? A man who fainted just because a girl poked him with a pencil didn't exactly seem the sort to successfully carry out a murder. Was it possible he hadn't been suffering from his current 'disorder' when he'd offed Mrs Fiske and those other people?

I was still trying to puzzle all of this out when Marcus, who'd shepherded me to the front door, produced my coat. He helped me into it, then said, 'Aikiku will drive you home, Miss Simon.'

I looked around and saw another Japanese guy, this one all in black, standing by the front door. He bowed politely to me.

'And let's get one thing straight.'

Marcus was still speaking to me in fatherly tones. He seemed irritated, but not really mad.

'What happened here tonight,' he went on, 'was very strange, it's true. But no one was injured . . .'

He must have noticed my gaze skitter towards Tad still passed out on the couch, since he added, 'Not seriously hurt, anyway. And so I think it would behove you to keep your mouth shut about what you've seen here. Because if you should take it into your head to tell anyone about what you've seen here,' Marcus went on in a manner one might almost call friendly, 'I will, of course, have to tell your parents about that unfortunate prank you played on Mr Beaumont . . . and press formal assault charges against you, of course.'

My mouth dropped open. I realized it, after a second, and snapped it shut again.

'But he—' I began.

Marcus cut me off. 'Did he?' He looked down at me

meaningfully. 'Did he really? There are no witnesses to that fact, save yourself. And do you really believe anyone is going to take the word of a little juvenile delinquent like yourself over the word of a respectable businessman?'

The jerk had me, and he knew it.

He smiled down at me, a little triumphant twinkle in his eye.

'Goodnight, Miss Simon,' he said.

Proving once again that the life of a mediator just ain't all it's cracked up to be: I didn't even get to stay for dessert.

Fifteen

Dropped off with about as much ceremony as a rolled-up newspaper on a Monday morning, I trudged up the driveway. I'd been a little scared Marcus had changed his mind about not pressing charges and that our house might have been surrounded by cops there to haul me in for assaulting Mr B.

But no one jumped out at me, gun drawn, from behind the bushes, which was a good sign.

As soon as I walked in, my mother was all over me, wanting to know what it had been like at the Beaumonts – What had we had for dinner? What had the decor been like? Had Tad asked me to the prom?

I declared myself too sleepy to talk and, instead, went straight up to my room. All I could think about was how on earth I was going to prove to the world that Red Beaumont was a cold-blooded killer.

Well, OK, maybe not a cold-blooded one, since he evidently felt remorse for what he'd done. But a killer, just the same.

I had forgotten, of course, about my new room-mate. As I approached my bedroom door, I saw Max sitting in front of it, his huge tongue lolling. There were scratch marks all up and down the door where he'd tried clawing his way in. I guess the fact that there was a cat in there was more over-powering than the fact that there was also a ghost in there.

'Bad dog,' I said when I saw the scratch marks.

Instantly, Doc's bedroom door across the hall opened.

'Have you got a cat in there?' he demanded, but not in an accusing way. More like he was really interested, from a scientific point of view.

'Um,' I said. 'Maybe.'

'Oh. I wondered. Because usually Max, you know, he stays away from your room. You know why.'

Doc widened his eyes meaningfully. When I'd first moved in, Doc had very chivalrously offered to trade rooms with me, since mine, he'd noted, had a distinct cold spot in it, a clear indication that it was a centre for paranormal activity. While I'd chosen to keep the room, I'd been impressed by Doc's self-sacrifice. His two elder brothers certainly hadn't been as generous.

'It's just for one night,' I assured him. 'The cat, I mean.'

'Oh,' Doc said. 'Well, that's good. Because you know that Brad does suffer from an adverse reaction to feline dander. Allergens, or allergy-producing substances, cause the release of histamine, an organic compound responsible for allergic symptoms. There are a variety of allergens, such as contac-tants – like poison oak – and airborne, like Brad's sensitivity to cat dander. The standard treatment is, of course, avoid-ance, if at all possible, of the allergen.'

I blinked at him. 'I'll keep that in mind,' I said.

Doc smiled. 'Great. Well, goodnight. Come on, Max.'

He hauled the dog away, and I went into my room.

To find that my new room-mate had flown the coop. Spike was gone, and the open window told me how he'd escaped.

'Jesse,' I muttered.

Jesse was always opening and closing my windows. I

hauled them open at night, only to find them securely closed come morning. Usually I appreciated this since the morning fog that rolled in from the bay was often freezing.

But now his good intentions had resulted in Spike escaping.

Well, I wasn't going looking for the stupid cat. If he wanted to come back, he knew the way. If not, I figured I'd done my duty, at least so far as Timothy was concerned. I'd found his wretched pet and brought it to safety. If the stupid thing refused to stay, that wasn't my problem.

I was just getting ready to climb into the hot, steaming bath I'd run for myself – I think best when submerged in soapy water – when the phone rang. I didn't answer it, of course, because the phone is hardly ever for me. It's usually either Debbie Mancuso – despite Dopey's protests that they were not seeing each other – or one of the multitudes of giggly young women who called for Sleepy . . . who was never home due to his gruelling pizza-delivery schedule.

This time, however, I heard my mother holler up the stairs that it was Father Dominic for me. My mother, in spite of what you might think, doesn't consider it the least bit weird that I am constantly getting phone calls from the principal of my school. Thanks to my being vice president of my class, and chairwoman of the Restore Junipero Serra's Head committee, there are actually quite a few completely innocuous reasons why the principal might need to call me.

But Father D never calls me at home to discuss anything remotely school related. He only calls when he wants to ream me out for something to do with mediating.

Before I picked up the extension in my room, I wondered – irritably, since I was wearing nothing but a towel and suspected my bath water would be cold by the time I finally got into it – what I had done this time.

And then, as if I'd already slid into that bath, and found it freezing, chills went up my spine.

Jesse. My hasty discussion with Jesse before I'd left for Tad's. Jesse had gone to Father Dominic.

No, he wouldn't have. I'd told him not to. Not unless I wasn't back by midnight. And I'd gotten home by ten. Earlier, even. Nine forty-five.

That couldn't be it, I told myself. That couldn't possibly be it. Father Dominic did not know about Jesse. He did not know a thing.

Still, when I said hello, I said it tentatively.

Father Dominic's voice was warm. 'Oh, hello, Susannah,' he gushed. 'So sorry to call so late, only I needed to discuss yesterday's student council meeting with you—'

'It's OK. Father D,' I said. 'My mom hung up the downstairs phone.'

Father Dominic's voice changed completely. It was no longer warm. Instead, it was very indignant.

'Susannah,' he said. 'Delighted as I am to find that you are all right, I would just like to know when, if ever, you were going to tell me about this Jesse person.'

Oops.

'He tells me he has been living in your bedroom since you moved to California several weeks ago, and that you have been perfectly aware, all this time, of that fact.'

I had to hold the phone away from my ear. I'd always known, of course, that Father Dominic would be mad when he found out about Jesse. But I never guessed he'd go ballistic.

'This is the most outrageous thing I've ever heard.' Father D was really warming to the subject. 'What would your poor mother say if she knew? I simply don't know what I'm going to do with you, Susannah. I thought you and I had

131

established a certain amount of trust in our relationship, but all this time, you've been keeping this Jesse fellow secret—'

Fortunately, at that moment, the call-waiting went off. I said, 'Oh, hold on a minute, would you, Father D?'

As I hit the receiver, I heard him say, 'Do not put me on hold while I am speaking to you, young lady—'

I'd been expecting Debbie Mancuso to be on the other line, but to my surprise, it was Cee Cee.

'Hey, Suze,' she said. 'I was doing a little more research on your boyfriend's dad—'

'He's not my boyfriend,' I said automatically. Especially not now.

'Yeah, OK, your would-be boyfriend, then. Anyway, I thought you might be interested to know that after his wife – Tad's mom – died ten years ago, things really started going downhill for Mr B.'

I raised my eyebrows. 'Downhill? Like how? Not financially. I mean, if you ever saw where they live . . .'

'No, not financially. I mean that after she died – breast cancer, diagnosed too late to treat; don't worry, nobody killed her – Mr B sort of lost interest in all of his many companies, and started keeping to himself.'

Aha. This was probably when the first onset of his 'disorder' began.

'Here's the really interesting part though,' Cee Cee said. I could hear her tapping on her keyboard. 'It was around this time that Red Beaumont handed over almost all of his responsibilities to his brother.'

'*Brother?*'

'Yeah. Marcus Beaumont.'

I was genuinely surprised. Marcus was *related* to Mr Beaumont? I'd thought him a mere flunky. But he wasn't. He was Tad's *uncle*.

'That's what it says. Mr Beaumont – Tad's dad – is still the figurehead, but this other Mr Beaumont is the one who's really been running things for the past ten years.'

I froze.

Oh my God. Had I got it wrong?

Maybe it hadn't been Red Beaumont at all who'd killed Mrs Fiske. Maybe it had been Marcus. The *other* Mr Beaumont.

Did Mr Beaumont kill you? That's what I'd asked Mrs Fiske. And she'd said yes. But Mr Beaumont to her might have been Marcus, not poor, vampire-wannabe Red Beaumont.

No, wait. Tad's father had told me straight out that he felt sorry for having killed all those people. That had been his motivation for inviting me over all along: he'd been hoping I'd help him communicate with his victims.

But Tad's father was clearly a couple of fries short of a Happy Meal. I don't think he could have killed a cockroach, let alone another human being.

No, whoever had killed Mrs Fiske and those other people had been smart enough to cover his tracks . . . and Tad's dad was no Daniel Boone, let me tell you.

His brother, on the other hand . . .

'I'm getting a really bad feeling about all this,' Cee Cee was saying. 'I mean, I know we can't prove anything – and despite what Adam thinks, it's highly unlikely anything my aunt Pru would have to contribute would be permissible in court – but I think we have a moral obligation—'

The call-waiting went off again. Father D. I'd forgotten all about Father D. He'd hung up in a rage and was calling back.

'Look, Cee Cee,' I said, still feeling sort of numb. 'We'll talk about it tomorrow at school, OK?'

'OK,' Cee Cee said. 'But I'm just letting you know, Suze, I think we've stumbled on to something big here.'

133

Big? Try gargantuan.

But it wasn't Father Dominic on the other line, I found out, after I pressed down on the receiver:

It was Tad.

'Sue?' he said. He still sounded a little groggy.

And he still seemed to have only a slight clue what my name was.

'Um, hi, Tad,' I said.

'Sue, I am so sorry,' he said. Grogginess aside, he sounded as if he meant it. 'I don't know what happened. I guess I was more tired than I thought. You know, at practice they run us pretty hard, and some nights I just conk out sooner than others . . .'

Yeah, I said to myself. I bet.

'Don't worry about it,' I said. Tad had way bigger things to concern himself with than falling asleep during a date.

'But I want to make it up to you,' Tad insisted. 'Please let me. What are you doing Saturday night?'

Saturday night? I forgot all about how this kid was related to a possible serial killer. What did *that* matter? He was asking me out. On a date. A *real* date. On Saturday night. Visions of candlelight and French kissing danced in my head. I could hardly speak, I was so flattered.

'I have a game,' Tad went on, 'but I figured you could come watch me play, and then afterwards we could maybe get a pizza with the rest of the guys or something.'

My excitement died a rapid little death.

Was he kidding? He wanted me to come watch him play *basketball?* Then go out with him and *the rest of the team?* For *pizza?* I wasn't even *burger* material? I mean, at this point, I'd settle for Sizzler, for crying out loud.

'Sue,' Tad said when I didn't say anything right away. 'You

134

aren't mad at me, are you? I mean, I really didn't mean to fall asleep on you.'

What was I thinking anyway? It would never work out between the two of us. I mean, I'm a mediator. His dad's a vampire. His uncle's a killer. What if we got married? Think how our kids would turn out . . .

Confused. Way confused.

Kind of like Tad.

'It wasn't that you were boring me or anything,' he went on. 'Really. Well, I mean, that thing you were talking about *was* kind of boring – the thing about that statue with the head that needed gluing back on. That story, I mean. But not *you*. *You're* not boring, Susan. That's not why I fell asleep, I swear it.'

'Tad,' I said, annoyed by how many times he'd felt it necessary to assure me I hadn't been boring him – a sure sign I'd been boring him senseless – and of course by the fact that he could not seem to remember my name. 'Grow up.'

He said, 'Whadduya mean?'

'I mean you didn't fall asleep, OK? You passed out because your dad slipped some Seconal or something into your coffee.'

OK, maybe that wasn't the most diplomatic way to tell the guy his father needed to up his meds. But hey, nobody's going to go around accusing me of being boring. *Nobody*.

Besides, don't you think he had a right to know?

'Sue,' he said, after a moment's pause. Pain throbbed in his voice. 'Why would you *say* something like that? I mean, how could you even *think* something like that?'

I guess I couldn't blame the poor guy. It was pretty hard to believe. Unless you'd seen it up close and personal the way I had.

'Tad,' I said. 'I mean it. Your old man . . . his phaser seems set on permanent stun, if you get my drift.'

'No,' Tad said, a little sullenly, I thought. 'I don't know what you're talking about.'

'Tad,' I said. 'Come on. The guy thinks he's a vampire.'

'He does not!' Tad, I realized, was up to his armpits in some major denial. 'You're full of it!'

I decided to show Tad just how full of it I was.

'No offence, buddy,' I said, 'but next time you're putting on one of those gold chains of yours, you might ask yourself where the money to pay for it came from. Or better yet, why don't you ask your uncle Marcus?'

'Maybe I will,' Tad said.

'Maybe you should,' I said.

'I will, then,' Tad said.

'Fine, then do it.'

I slammed down the phone. Then I sat there staring down at it.

What on earth had I just done?

Sixteen

In spite of the fact that I'd nearly killed a man that night, I didn't have too many problems falling asleep.

Seriously.

OK, so I was tired, all right? I mean, let's face it: I'd had a trying day.

And it wasn't like those phone calls I'd gotten just before I'd gone to bed had helped. Father Dominic was totally mad at me for not having told him sooner about Jesse, and Tad seemed to pretty much hate me now too.

Oh, and his uncle Marcus? Yeah, possible serial killer. Almost forgot that part.

But seriously, what was I supposed to do? I mean, I'd known perfectly well Father D wasn't going to be thrilled about Jess. And as for Tad, well, if my dad had ever drugged me stupid, I would totally want to know.

I'd done the right thing telling Tad.

Except I did sort of wonder what was going to happen if Tad really did go ask his uncle Marcus what I'd meant about where his money came from. Marcus would probably think it was some obscure reference to Tad's father's mental illness.

I hoped.

Because if he figured out that I suspected the truth – you know, that whole thing about his killing anyone who stood in the way of Beaumont Industries gobbling up as much of the available property in northern California that it possibly could – I had a feeling he wasn't going to take too kindly to it.

But how scared would a big-time player like Marcus Beaumont be of a sixteen-year-old schoolgirl? I mean, really. He had no idea about the whole mediator thing, how I'd actually spoken to one of his victims and confirmed the whole thing.

Well, more or less.

Still, in spite of all that, I did finally get to sleep. I was dreaming that Kelly Prescott had heard about Tad and me being at the Coffee Clutch together, and that she was threatening to veto the decision not to have a spring dance in revenge when a soft *thud* woke me. I raised my head and squinted in the direction of the window seat.

Spike was back. And he had company.

Jesse, I saw, was sitting next to Spike. To my utter amazement the cat was letting him pet him. That stupid cat who had tried to bite me every time I'd come near him was letting a ghost – his natural enemy – pet him.

And what's more, Spike seemed to *like* it. He was purring so loud I could hear him all the way across the room.

'Whoa,' I said, leaning up on my elbows. '*That* is one for *Ripley's Believe It or Not.*'

Jesse grinned at me. 'I think he likes me,' he said.

'Don't get too attached. He can't stay here, you know.'

I could have sworn Jesse looked crestfallen. 'Why not?'

'Because Dopey's allergic, for one thing,' I said. 'And because I didn't even ask anyone if it was OK for me to have a cat.'

'It is your house now, as well as your brothers',' Jesse said with a shrug.

'Stepbrothers,' I corrected him. I thought about what he said, then added, 'And I guess I still feel like more of a guest here than an actual occupant.'

'Give yourself a century or so.' He grinned some more. 'And you'll get over it.'

'Very funny,' I said. 'Besides, that cat hates me.'

'I'm sure he doesn't hate you,' Jesse said.

'Yes, he does. Every time I come near him, he tries to bite me.'

'He just doesn't know you,' Jesse said. 'I will introduce you.' He picked up the cat and pointed him in my direction. 'Cat,' he said. 'This is Susannah. Susannah, meet the cat.'

'Spike,' I said.

'I beg your pardon?'

'Spike. That cat's name is Spike.'

Jesse put the cat down and looked at him in horror. 'That is a terrible name for a cat.'

'Yeah,' I said. Then I added – strictly conversationally, if you know what I mean – 'So I hear you met Father Dominic.'

Jesse raised his gaze and let it rest expressionlessly on me. 'Why didn't you tell him about me, Susannah?'

I swallowed. What do they do, teach guys that reproach-ful look at birth or something? I mean, they all seem to have it down so pat. Except Dopey, that is.

'Look,' I said. 'I *wanted* to. Only I knew he was going to freak out. I mean, he's a priest. I didn't figure he'd be too thrilled to hear that I've got a guy – even a dead guy – living in my bedroom.' I tried to sound as concerned as I felt. 'So, um, I take it you two didn't hit it off?'

'Between your father and the priest,' Jesse said wryly, 'I would take your father any time.'

'Well,' I said. 'Don't worry about it. Tomorrow I'll just tell

Father Dom about all the times you saved my life, and then he'll just have to deal.'

He clearly didn't believe it was going to be that simple if the scowl that appeared on his face was any indication. The sad thing was, he was right. Father D wasn't going to be mollified that easily, and we both knew it.

'Look.' I threw back the covers and got up out of bed, padding over to the window seat in my boxers and T-shirt. 'I'm sorry. I'm really sorry, Jesse. I should have told him sooner and introduced the two of you properly. It's my fault.'

'It isn't your fault,' Jesse said.

'Yes, it is.' I sat down next to him, making sure Jesse was between myself and the cat. 'I mean, you may be dead, but I haven't got any right to treat you as if you were. That's just plain rude. Maybe what we can do is, you and me and Father Dom can all sit down and have lunch together or something, and then he can see what a nice guy you really are.'

Jesse looked at me like I was a mental case. 'Susannah,' he said. 'I don't eat, remember?'

'Oh, yeah. I forgot.'

Spike butted Jesse in the arm, and he lifted his hand and began scratching the cat's ears. I felt so bad for Jesse – I mean, think about it: he had been hanging around in that house for a *hundred and fifty years* before I'd gotten there, with no one to talk to, no one at all – that I suddenly blurted out, 'Jesse, if there was any way I could make you not dead, I'd do it.'

He smiled, but at the cat, not at me. 'Would you?'

'In a minute,' I said, and then went on, with complete recklessness, 'Except that if you weren't dead, you probably wouldn't want to hang out with me.'

That made him look at me. He said, 'Of course I would.'

'No,' I said, examining one of my bare knees in the moonlight. 'You wouldn't. If you weren't dead, you'd be in college or something, and you'd want to hang around with college girls, and not boring high-school girls like me.'

Jesse said, 'You aren't boring.'

'Oh, yes, I am,' I assured him. 'You've just been dead so long, you don't know it.'

'Susannah,' he said. 'I know it, all right?'

I shrugged. 'You don't have to try to make me feel better. It's OK. I've come to accept it. There are some things you just can't change.'

'Like being dead,' Jesse said quietly.

Well, *that* certainly put a damper on things. I was feeling kind of depressed about everything – the fact that Jesse was dead, and that in spite of this, Spike still liked him better than me, and stuff like that – when all of a sudden Jesse reached out and took hold of my chin – almost exactly the way Tad had that night in his car – between his index finger and thumb and turned my face toward his.

And things suddenly started looking up.

Instead of collapsing in shock – my first instinct – I lifted my gaze to his face. The moonlight that had been filtering into my room through the bay windows was reflected in Jesse's soft dark eyes, and I could feel the heat from his fingers coursing through me.

That's when I realized that in spite of how hard I'd been trying to not to fall in love with Jesse, I wasn't doing a very good job. I could tell this by the way my heart started thudding very hard against my T-shirt when he touched me. It hadn't done that when Tad had touched me in the exact same way.

And I could also tell by the way I instantly started worrying about the fact that he had chosen this particular moment to kiss me, the middle of the night, when it had been hours since I'd brushed my teeth and I was sure I probably had morning breath. How appetizing was that?

But I never discovered whether or not Jesse would have been grossed out by my morning breath – or even if he'd really been going to kiss me at all – because at that moment, that crazy woman who kept insisting Red hadn't killed her suddenly showed up again, shrieking her head off.

I swear I nearly jumped a foot. She was the last person I'd been expecting to see.

'Oh, my God,' I cried, slapping my hands over my ears as she let loose like some kind of smoke detector. 'What's the matter?'

The woman had been wearing the hood of her grey sweatshirt. Now she pushed it back, and in the moonlight, I could see the tears that had made tracks down her thin, pale cheeks. I couldn't believe I had mistaken her for Mrs Fiske. This woman was years and years younger, and a heck of a lot prettier.

'You didn't tell him,' she said, between sobbing wails.

I blinked. 'Yes, I did.'

'You didn't!'

'No, I did, I really did.' I was shocked by this unfair accusation. 'I told him a couple of days ago. Jesse, tell her.'

'She told him,' Jesse assured the dead woman.

You would think one ghost would take the word of another. But she wasn't having any of it. She cried, 'You *didn't*! And you've *got* to tell him. You've just *got* to. It's tearing him up inside.'

'Wait a minute,' I said. 'Red Beaumont *is* the Red you're talking about, right? Isn't he the one who killed you?'

She shook her head so hard, her hair smacked her cheeks and then stuck there, glued to her skin by her tears. 'No,' she said. 'No! I told you Red *didn't* do it.'

'Marcus, I mean,' I amended, quickly. 'I know Red didn't do it. He just blames himself for it, right? That's what you want me to tell him. That it wasn't his fault. It was his brother, Marcus Beaumont, who killed you, wasn't it?'

'No!' She looked at me like I was a moron. And I was starting to feel like one. 'Not Red *Beaumont*. Red. *Red! You know him.*'

I know him? I know someone named Red? Not in this life.

'Look,' I said. 'I need a little more info than that. Why don't we start with introductions. I'm Susannah Simon, OK? And you are . . . ?'

The look she gave me would have broken the heart of even the coldest mediator.

'You *know*,' she said, with an expression so wounded, I had to look away. 'You *know* . . .'

And then, when I risked another glance in her direction, she was gone again.

'Um,' I said, uncomfortably, to Jesse. 'I guess I got the wrong Red.'

Seventeen

OK, I admit it: I wasn't happy.

I mean, seriously. I had invested all that time and effort in Red Beaumont, and he hadn't even been the right guy.

OK, yeah, so he – or his brother; my money was on his brother – had apparently killed a bunch of people, but I'd stumbled over this fact completely by accident. The ghost who'd originally come to me for help didn't have anything to do with Red Beaumont or even with his brother, Marcus. Her message remained undelivered because I couldn't figure out who she was, even though, apparently, I knew her.

And meanwhile, Mrs Fiske's killer was still walking around free.

And as if all of that weren't enough, my midnight caller showing up the way she did had completely killed the mood between Jesse and me. He so totally did not kiss me after that. In fact, he acted like he'd never intended to kiss me in the first place, which, considering my luck, is probably the truth. Instead, he asked how my poison oak was progressing.

My poison oak! Yeah, thanks, it's great.

God, I am such a loser.

But you know, I pretended like I didn't care. I got up the next morning and acted like nothing had happened. I put on my best butt-kicking outfit – my black Betsey Johnson miniskirt with black ribbed tights, side-zip Batgirl boots and purple Armani sweater set – and strutted around my room like all I was thinking about was how I was going to bring Marcus Beaumont to justice. The last thing on my mind, I pretended, was Jesse.

Not like he noticed. He wasn't even around.

But all my strutting around had made me late, and Sleepy was standing at the bottom of the stairs bellowing my name, so even if he'd wanted to, it wouldn't have been such a good thing for Jesse to materialize just then anyway.

I grabbed my leather jacket and came pounding down the stairs to where Andy was standing shelling out lunch money to each of us as we came by.

'My goodness, Suze,' he said when he saw me.

'*What?*' I demanded defensively.

'Nothing,' he said quickly. 'Here.'

I plucked the five-dollar bill from his hand and, casting him one last, curious glance, followed Doc down to the car. When I got there, Dopey took one look at me and let out a howl.

'Oh, my God,' he cried, pointing at me. 'Run for your lives!'

I narrowed my eyes at him.

'Do you have a problem?' I asked him coldly.

'Yeah, I do,' he sneered at me. 'I didn't know it was Hallowe'en.'

Doc said knowingly, 'It isn't Hallowe'en, Brad. Hallowe'en isn't for another two hundred and seventy-nine days.'

'Tell that to the Queen of the Undead,' Dopey said.

I don't know what made me do it. I was in a bad mood, I guess. Everything that had happened the night before, from stabbing Mr Beaumont to finding out I'd had the wrong man all along – not to mention my discovery that my feelings about Jesse weren't exactly what I'd have liked them to be – came back to me.

And the next thing I knew, I'd turned around and sunk my fist into Dopey's stomach.

He let out a groan and pitched forwards, then sprawled out into the grass, gasping for air.

OK, I admit it. I felt bad. I shouldn't have done it.

But still. What a baby. I mean, seriously. He's on the wrestling team. What are they teaching these wrestlers anyway? Clearly not how to take a punch.

'Whoa,' Sleepy said when he noticed that Dopey was on the ground. 'What the hell happened to you?'

Dopey pointed at me, trying to say my name. But all that came out were gasps.

'Aw, Jesus,' Sleepy said, looking at me disgustedly.

'He called me,' I said, with all the dignity I could muster, 'the Queen of the Undead.'

Sleepy said, 'Well, what do you expect him to say? You look like a hooker. Sister Ernestine's going to send you home if she sees you in that skirt.'

I sucked in my breath, outraged. 'This skirt,' I said, 'happens to be by Betsey Johnson.'

'I don't care if it's by Betsy Ross. And neither will Sister Ernestine. Come on, Brad, get up. We're going to be late.'

Brad got up with elaborate care, as if every movement was causing him excruciating pain. Sleepy didn't look as if he felt too sorry for him. 'I told you not to mess with her, sport,' was all he said as he slid behind the wheel.

'She sucker-punched me, man,' Brad whined. 'She can't get away with that.'

'Actually,' Doc said pleasantly, as he climbed into the back seat and fastened his seat belt, 'she can. While statistics concerning domestic violence are always difficult to obtain due to low reportage, incidents in which females batter male family members are reported even less, as the victims are almost always too embarrassed to tell members of law enforcement that they have, in fact, been beaten by a woman.'

'Well, I'm not embarrassed,' Dopey declared. 'I'm telling Dad as soon as we get home.'

'Go ahead,' I said acidly. I was in a really bad mood. 'He's just going to ground you again when I tell him you went ahead and snuck out that night of Kelly Prescott's pool party.'

'I did not,' he practically screamed in my face.

'Then how is it,' I inquired, 'that I saw you in her pool house giving Debbie Mancuso's tongue a Jiffy Lube?'

Even Sleepy hooted at that one.

Dopey, completely red with embarrassment, looked as if he might start crying. I licked my finger and made a little slashing motion in the air as if I were writing on a scoreboard. Suze, one. Dopey, zero.

But Dopey, unfortunately, was the one who had the last laugh.

We were approaching our lines for Assembly – they seriously make every single grade stand outside the school in these lines separated by sex, boys on one side, girls on the other, for fifteen minutes before class officially starts, so they can take attendance and read announcements – when Sister Ernestine blew her whistle at me, and signalled for me to come over to her, where she was standing by the flagpole.

Fortunately, she did this in front of the entire sophomore class – not to mention the freshmen – so that every single one of my peers had the privilege of seeing me get bawled out by a nun for wearing a miniskirt to school.

The upshot of it all was that Sister Ernestine said I had to go home and change.

Oh, I argued. I insisted that a society that valued its members solely for their outward appearance was a society destined for destruction, which was a line I'd heard Doc use a few days earlier when she'd busted him for wearing Levis – there's a strict anti-jeans rule at the Academy.

But Sister Ernestine didn't go for it. She informed me that I could go home and change, or I could sit in her office and help grade the second graders' maths quizzes until my mother arrived with a pair of slacks for me.

Oh, that wouldn't be *too* embarrassing.

Given the alternative, I elected to go home and change – although I argued strenuously on behalf of Ms Johnson and her designs. A skirt, however, with a hem higher than three inches above the knee is not considered appropriate Academy attire. And my skirt, unfortunately, was more than four inches above my knees. I know because Sister Ernestine took out a ruler and showed me. And the rest of the sopho-more class as well.

And so it was that, with a wave to Cee Cee and Adam, who were leading the class's shouts of encouragement to me – which fortunately drowned out the catcalls Dopey and his friends were making – I shouldered my backpack and left the school grounds. I had, of course, to walk home, since I could not face the indignity of calling Andy for a ride, and I still hadn't figured out whether or not there was such a thing as public transportation in Carmel.

I wasn't too deeply bummed. After all, what had I had to look forward to? Oh, just Father Dominic reaming me out for not telling him about Jesse. I could, I suppose, have dis-tracted him by telling him how wrong he'd been about Tad's dad being a vampire – he just *thinks* he's one – and what Cee

Cee had discovered about his brother, Marcus. That certainly would have gotten him off my back . . . for a little while anyway.

But then what? So a couple of environmentalists were missing? That didn't prove anything. So a dead lady had told me a Mr Beaumont had killed her? Oh, yeah, that'd stand up in court, all right.

Not a lot to go on. We had, in fact, nothing. Nada. Zilch.

Which was what I was feeling like as I strolled along. A big miniskirted zero.

As if whoever was in charge of the weather agreed with me about my loser status, it was sort of raining. It was foggy every morning along the coast in northern California. The fog rolled in from the sea and sat in the bay until the sun burned it all off.

But this morning, on top of the fog, there was this light drizzle coming down. It wasn't so bad at first, but I hadn't gotten further than the school gates before my hair started curling up. After all the time I'd spent that morning straightening it. I didn't, of course, have an umbrella. Nor, it seemed, did I have much of a choice. I was going to be a drenched, curly-haired freak by the time I walked the two miles – mostly uphill – to the house, and that was the end of it.

Or so I thought. Because as I was passing the school gates, a car pulling in between them slowed.

It was a nice car. It was an expensive car. It was a black car with smoked windows. As I looked at it one of those windows lowered and a familiar face peered out at me from the backseat.

'Miss Simon,' Marcus Beaumont said pleasantly. 'Just the person I was looking for. May I have a word?'

And he opened the passenger door invitingly, beckoning for me to come in out of the rain.

Every single one of my mediator neurons fired at once. Danger, they screamed. Run for it, they shrieked.

I couldn't believe it. Tad had done it. Tad had asked his uncle what I'd meant.

And Marcus, instead of shrugging it off, had come here to my school in a car with smoked windows to 'have a word' with me.

I was dead meat.

But before I had a chance to spin around and hightail back into the school, where I knew I'd be safe, the passenger doors of Marcus Beaumont's sedan sprang open and these two guys came at me.

Let me just say in my defence that deep down, I never thought Tad would have the guts to do it. I mean. Tad seemed like a nice enough guy, and God knew he was a great kisser, but he didn't seem to be the sharpest knife in the drawer, if you know what I mean. This, I imagine, is why a girl like Kelly Prescott would find him so appealing: Kelly's used to being the Wusthof. She doesn't welcome competition in that capacity.

But I had obviously underestimated Tad. Not only had he gone to his uncle as I'd suggested, but he'd evidently managed to raise Marcus's suspicions that I knew more than I'd let on.

Way more if the two thugs who were circling me, cutting off any possible chance at escape, were any indication.

My option for flight pretty much voided by these two clowns, I saw that I was going to have to fight. I do not consider myself a slouch in the fighting department. I actually kind of like it, if you haven't figured that out already. Of course, usually I'm fighting ghosts, and not live human beings. But if you think about it, there's not really that much of a difference. I mean, nasal cartilage is nasal cartilage. I was willing to give it a go.

This seemed to come as something of a surprise to Marcus's flunkies. A couple of thickset frat boys who looked as if they were better used to pounding brewskies than people, they were out to impress the boss in a big way.

At least until I threw down my book bag, hooked my foot behind the knee of one them, and brought him down with a ground-shaking thud to the wet asphalt.

While Thug #1 lay there staring up at the overcast sky with a surprised look on his face, I got in an excellent kick to Thug #2. He was too tall for me to get him in the nose, but I knocked the wind out of him by applying my three-inch heel to his rib cage. That had to have hurt, let me tell you. He went spinning around, lost his balance, and hit the ground.

Amateur.

Marcus got out of the car then. He stood with the rain beating down on his fluffy blond hair and went, 'You idiot,' to Thug #2.

He was right to be upset, if you think about it. I mean, he'd hired these guys to roust me, and they were doing a thoroughly bad job of it. It just goes to show you can't get good help any more.

You would think that, with all this going on in front of a pretty popular tourist destination like the Mission – not to mention a *school* – somebody would have noticed and phoned the cops. You would think that, wouldn't you?

But if you're thinking that, you obviously haven't been in California when it was raining out. I'm not kidding, it's like New York City on New Year's Eve: only the tourists venture outside. Everyone else stays inside and waits until it's safe to come out.

Oh, a couple of cars whizzed by going fifty miles an hour in a twenty-mile-per-hour zone. I was hoping one of them would notice us and decide that two guys on one girl wasn't quite playing fair – even if the girl did look a bit like a hooker.

But our little tussle went on for a surprisingly long time before Marcus – who'd apparently realized what his thugs hadn't, that I wasn't exactly your typical Catholic schoolgirl – cut the whole thing short by laying me out with a totally unfair right to the chin.

I didn't even see him coming. What with the rain and all, my hair was getting plastered to my face, obscuring my peripheral vision. I'd been concentrating on applying a knee to Thug #1's groin – it had been a bad idea, his decision to get up again – while keeping my eye on Thug #2, who kept grabbing for handfuls of my hair – he had obviously gone to the Dopey school of fighting – and hadn't even noticed that Marcus was headed my way.

But suddenly, a heavy hand landed on my shoulder and spun me around. A second later, an explosion sounded in my head. The world tilted sickeningly, and I felt myself stumble. Next thing I knew, I was inside the car, and brakes were squealing.

'Ow,' I said when the stars I'd been seeing had receded enough for me to speak. I reached up and touched my jaw. None of my teeth felt loose, but I was definitely going to have a bruise that there wasn't enough Clinique in the world to cover up. 'What'd you have to hit me so hard for?'

Marcus just blinked at me expressionlessly from where he sat on the seat beside me. Thug #1 was driving and Thug #2 sat beside him in the front seat. Judging from the backs of their extremely thick necks, they were unhappy. It couldn't have been too pleasant sitting there with all those various body parts throbbing with pain, in wet, muddy clothes. My leather jacket had fortunately protected me from the worst of the rain. My hair, however, was undoubtedly a lost cause. –

We were going fast down the highway. Water sluiced on either side of us as we barrelled through what had become a steady downpour. There wasn't a soul on the highway but us. I tell you, you've never seen people as scared of a little bit of rain as native Californians. Earthquakes? They're nothing. But a hint of drizzle and it's head-between-the-knees time.

'Look,' I said. 'I think you should know something. My mother is a reporter for WCAL in Monterey, and if anything happens to me, she is going to be all over you like ants on a Jolly Rancher.'

Marcus, clearly bored by my posturing, pulled back his coat sleeve and looked at his Rolex. 'She won't,' he said, tonelessly. 'No one knows where you are. It was quite fortuitous, your leaving the school at the very moment we were pulling up to it. Did another one of your *ghosts* –' he said the word with a sarcasm I suppose he found scathing – 'warn you that we were coming?'

Scowling, I muttered, 'Not exactly.' No way was I going to tell him I'd been sent home for violating the school dress code. I'd been humiliated enough for one day.

'Just what were *you* doing there anyway?' I demanded. 'I mean, were you just going to stroll in and yank me out of class at gunpoint in front of everyone?'

'Certainly not,' Marcus said calmly.

What I was hoping was that somebody – anybody – had seen Marcus slug me and had taken down the licence number of his expensive Euro-trash car. Any minute sirens might begin to wail behind us. The *cops* couldn't be afraid of a little rain – although to tell the truth, I don't remember

CHiPs officers Ponch and Jon ever venturing out in a down-pour . . .

Keep him talking, I told myself. If he's talking, he won't be able to concentrate on killing you.

'So what was the plan, then?'

'If you must know, I was going to go to the principal and inform him that Beaumont Industries was interested in sponsoring a student's tuition for the year, and that you were one of our finalists.' Marcus picked some invisible lint off his trouser leg. 'We would, of course, require a personal interview, after which we intended to take you – the candidate – to a celebratory lunch.'

I rolled my eyes. The idea of me winning any kind of scholarship was laughable. This guy obviously hadn't seen my latest Geometry quiz scores.

'Father Dominic would never have let me go with you,' I said. Especially, I thought, after I'd filled him in on what had gone on at chez Beaumont the night before.

'Oh, I think he might have. I was planning on making a sizeable donation to his little mission.'

I had to laugh at that one. This guy obviously didn't know Father D at all.

'I don't think so,' I said. 'And even if he did, don't you think he would mention how the last time he saw me, I was going off in a car with you? If the cops should happen to question him, you know, after I disappeared, that is.'

Marcus said, 'Oh, you're not going to disappear, Miss Simon.'

This surprised me. 'I'm not?' Then what was all this about?

'Oh, no,' Marcus assured me confidently. 'There won't be the slightest question about what's happened to you. Your corpse is going to be found rather quickly, I imagine.'

Eighteen

This was so not what I wanted to hear, I can't even tell you.

'Look,' I said quickly. 'I think you should know that I left a letter with a friend of mine. If anything happens to me, she's supposed to go to the cops and give it to them.'

I smiled sunnily at him. Of course, it was all a big fat lie, but he didn't know that.

Or maybe he did.

'I don't think so,' he said politely.

I shrugged, pretending I didn't care. 'Your funeral.'

'You really,' Marcus said, as I was busy straining my ears for sirens, 'oughtn't to have tipped off the boy. That was your first mistake, you know.'

Didn't I know it.

'Well,' I said. 'I thought he had a right to know what his own father was up to.'

Marcus looked a little disappointed in me. 'I didn't mean that,' he said, and there was just a hint of contempt in his voice.

'What, then?' I opened my eyes as wide as they would go. Little Miss Innocent.

'I wasn't certain you knew about me, of course,' Marcus went on, almost amiably. 'Not until you tried to run back there, in front of the school. That, of course, was your second mistake. Your evident fear of me was a dead give-away. Because then there was no question that you knew more than was good for you.'

'Yeah, but look,' I said, in my most reasonable voice. 'What was it you said last night? Who's going to believe the word of a sixteen-year-old juvenile delinquent like myself over a big important businessman like you? I mean, please. You're friends with the governor, for crying out loud.'

'And your mother,' Marcus reminded me, 'is a reporter with WCAL, as you pointed out.'

Me and my big mouth.

The car, which had showed no signs of slowing down up until that point, started rounding a curve in the road. We were, I realized suddenly, on Seventeen Mile Drive.

I didn't even think about what I was doing. I just reached for the door handle, and the next thing I knew, a guard rail was looming at me, and rainwater and gravel were splashing up into my face.

But instead of rolling out of the car and up against that guard rail – below which I could see the roiling waves of the Restless Sea crashing against the boulders that rested at the bottom of the cliff we were on – I stayed where I was. That was because Marcus grabbed the back of my leather jacket and wouldn't let go.

'Not so fast,' he said, trying to haul me back into the seat.

I wasn't giving up so easily though. I twisted around – quite nimble in my Lycra skirt – and tried to slam my boot heel into his face. Unfortunately, Marcus's reflexes were as good as mine since he caught my foot and twisted it very painfully.

'Hey,' I yelled. 'That hurt!'

But Marcus just laughed and clocked me again.

Let me tell you, that didn't feel so swell. For a minute or

so, I couldn't see too straight. It was during this moment that it took for my vision to adjust that Marcus closed the passenger door, which had continued to yawn open, stowed me back into my place, and buckled me safely in. When my eyeballs finally settled back into their sockets, I looked down, and saw that he was keeping a firm hold on me, primarily by clutching a handful of my sweater set.

'Hello,' I said feebly. 'That's cashmere, you know.'

Marcus said, 'I will release you if you promise to be reasonable.'

'I think it's perfectly reasonable,' I said, 'to try to escape from a guy like you.'

Marcus didn't look very impressed by my sensible take on the matter.

'You can't possibly imagine that I'm going to let you go,' he said. 'I've got damage control to worry about. I mean, I can't have you going around telling people about my, er . . . unique problem-solving techniques.'

'There's nothing very unique,' I informed him, 'about murder.'

Marcus said, as if I hadn't spoken, 'Historically, you understand, there have always been an ignorant few who have insisted upon standing in the way of progress. These are the people I was forced to . . . relocate.'

'Yeah,' I said. 'To their graves.'

Marcus shrugged. 'Unfortunate, certainly, but nevertheless necessary. Still, in order for us to advance as a civilization, sacrifices must occasionally be made by a select few—'

'I doubt Mrs Fiske agrees with who you selected to be sacrificed,' I interrupted.

'What may appear to one party to be improvement may appear to another to be wanton destruction—'

'Like the annihilation of our natural coastline by money-grubbing parasites like yourself?'

Well, he'd already said he was going to kill me. I didn't figure it mattered whether or not I was polite to him.

'And so for progress – real progress,' he went on, as if he hadn't even heard me, 'to be made, some simply have to do without.'

'Without their *lives*?' I glared at him. 'Dude, let me tell you something. You know your brother, the wannabe-vampire? You are every bit as sick as he is.'

The car, right at that moment, pulled into the driveway of Mr Beaumont's house. The guard at the gate waved to as we went by, though he couldn't see me through the tinted windows. He probably had no idea that inside his boss's car was a teenage girl who was about to be executed. No one – *no one* – I realized, knew where I was: not my mother, not Father Dominic, not Jesse – not even my dad. I had no idea what Marcus had planned for me, but whatever it was, I suspected I wasn't going to like it very much . . . especially if it got me where it had gotten Mrs Fiske.

Which I was beginning to think it probably would.

The car pulled to a halt. Marcus's fingers bit into my upper arm.

'Come on,' he said, and he started dragging me across the seat towards his side of the car and the open passenger door.

'Wait a minute,' I said, in a last ditch effort to convince him that I could be perfectly reasonable given the right incentive – for instance, being killed. 'What if I promised not to tell anyone?'

'You already have told someone,' Marcus reminded me. 'My nephew, Tad, remember?'

'Tad won't tell anyone. He can't. He's related to you. He's not allowed to testify against his own relatives in court, or something.' My head was still kind of wobbly from the smack Marcus had given me, so I wasn't at my most lucid. Nevertheless, I tried my best to reason with him. 'Tad is a super secret keeper.'

'The dead,' Marcus reminded me, 'usually are.'

If I hadn't been scared before – and I most definitely had been – I was super scared now. What did he mean by that? Did he mean . . . did he mean Tad wouldn't talk because he'd be dead? This guy was going to kill his own nephew? Because of what *I'd* told him?

I couldn't let that happen. I had no idea what Marcus intended to do with me, but one thing I knew for sure:

He wasn't going to lay a finger on my boyfriend.

Although at that particular moment, I had no idea how I was going to prevent him from doing so.

As Marcus yanked on me, I said to his thugs, 'I just want to thank you guys for helping me out. You know, considering I'm a defenceless young girl and this guy is a cold-blooded killer, and all. Really. You've been great—'

Marcus gave me a jerk and I came flying out of the car towards him.

'Whoa,' I said, when I'd found my feet. 'What's with the rough stuff?'

'I'm not taking any chances,' Marcus said, keeping his iron grip on my arm as he dragged me towards the front door of the house. 'You've proved a good deal more trouble than I ever anticipated.'

Before I had time to digest this compliment, Marcus had hauled me into the house while behind us the thugs got out of the car and followed along . . . just in case, I suppose, I suddenly broke free and tried to pull a *La Femme Nikita*-type escape.

Inside the Beaumonts' house – from what I could see

159

given the speed with which Marcus was dragging me around – things were much the same as they'd been the last time I'd visited. There was no sign of Mr Beaumont – he was probably in bed recovering from my brutal attack on him the night before. Poor thing, If I'd known it was Marcus who was the bloodsucking parasite and not his brother, I'd have shown the old guy a little compassion.

Which reminded me.

'What about Tad?' I asked as Marcus steered me across the patio, where rain was pattering into the pool, making hundreds of little splashes and thousands of ripples. 'Where've you got him locked up?'

'You'll see,' Marcus assured me as he pulled me into the little corridor where the elevator to Mr Beaumont's office sat.

He threw open the elevator door and pushed me inside the little moving room, then joined me there. His thugs took up positions in the hallway since there was no room for them and their overmuscled girth in the elevator. I was glad because Thug #1's wool peacoat had been starting to smell a little ripe.

Once again, I had a sensation of moving, but couldn't trace whether it was up or down. As we rode, I had a chance to study Marcus up close and personal. It was funny, but he really looked like an ordinary guy. He could have been anyone, a travel agent, a lawyer, a doctor.

But he wasn't. He was a murderer.

How proud his mom must be.

'You know,' I remarked, 'when my mom finds out about this, Beaumont Industries is going down. Way down.'

'She's not going to connect your death with Beaumont Industries,' Marcus informed me.

'Oh, yeah? Dude, let me tell you something. The minute

160

my mutilated corpse is found, my mom's gonna turn into that creature from *Aliens 2*. You know the one where Sigourney Weaver gets into that forklift thing? And then—'

'You aren't going to be mutilated,' Marcus snapped. He was obviously not a movie buff. He flung open the elevator door, and I saw that we were back where all of this had started, in Mr Beaumont's spooky office.

'You're going,' he said, with satisfaction, 'to drown.'

Nineteen

'Here.'

Marcus, by applying steady pressure to the small of my back, had steered me into the middle of the room. He went around the desk, reached into a drawer, and pulled out something red and silky. He threw it at me.

I, with my lightning quick reflexes, caught it, dropped it, then picked it up and squinted down at it. Except for the lights at the bottom of the aquarium, the room was in darkness.

'Put it on,' Marcus said.

It was a bathing suit. A Speedo one-piece. I tossed it, as if it had burned my fingers, on to the top of Red Beaumont's desk.

'No thanks,' I said. 'Racerback straps don't really do it for me.'

Marcus sighed. His gaze strayed towards the wall to my right. 'Tad,' he said, 'wasn't nearly so difficult to persuade as you.'

I spun around. Stretched out on a leather sofa I hadn't noticed before lay Tad. He was either asleep or unconscious. My vote was for unconscious, since most people don't nod off in their swimwear.

That's right: Tad was sans apparel, save for those swim

162

trunks I'd been lucky enough to have seen him in once before.

I turned back towards his uncle Marcus.

'Nobody's going to believe it,' I said. 'I mean, it's raining outside. Nobody's going to believe we'd go swimming in weather like this.'

'You aren't going swimming,' Marcus said. He'd wandered over towards the aquarium. Now he tapped on the glass to get the attention of an angel fish. 'You're taking out my brother's yacht, and then you're going jet-skiing.'

'In the *rain*?'

Marcus looked at me pityingly. 'You've never been jet-skiing before, have you?'

Actually, no. I prefer to keep my feet, whenever possible, on dry land. Preferably in Prada, but I'll settle for Nine West.

'The water is particularly choppy in weather like this,' Marcus explained patiently. 'Seasoned jet-skiers – like my nephew – can't get enough of the whitecaps. On the whole, it's the perfect kind of activity for a couple of thrill-seeking teenagers who have cut school to enjoy one another's company . . . and who will, of course, never make it back to shore. Well, not alive anyway.'

Marcus sighed, and went on, 'You see, regrettably, Tad refuses to wear a life vest when he goes out on the water – much too restricting – and I'm afraid he's going to convince you to go without as well. The two of you will stray too far from the boat, a particularly strong swell will knock you over, and . . . Well, the currents will probably toss your lifeless body to shore eventually—' He pulled up his sleeve and glanced at his watch again. 'Most likely tomorrow morning. Now hurry and change. I have a lunch appointment with a gentleman who wants to sell me a piece of property that would be perfect for a Chuck E. Cheese.'

'You can't kill your own *nephew*.' My voice cracked. I was truly feeling . . . well, horrified. 'I mean, I can't imagine something like that is going to make you too popular at Grandma's around the holidays.'

Marcus's mouth set into a grim line. 'Perhaps you didn't understand me. As I have just taken great pains to explain to you, Miss Simon, your death, as well as my nephew's, is going to look like a tragic accident.'

'Is this how you got rid of Mrs Fiske?' I demanded. 'Jet-ski accident?'

'Hardly,' he said, rolling his eyes. 'I wasn't interested in having her body found. Without a body there's no proof a murder has taken place, correct? Now, be a good girl and—'

This guy was a complete mental case. I mean, Red Beaumont, for all his believing he's from Transylvania, isn't anywhere near as cuckoo for Cocoa Puffs as his little brother.

'Is this how you get your kicks?' I glared at him. 'You really are a sicko. And for your information, I am *not*,' I declared, 'taking a stitch off. Whoever finds this body is going to find it fully clothed, thank you very much.'

'Oh, I *am* sorry,' he said. He actually sounded apologetic. 'Of course you'd like a little privacy while you change. You'll have to forgive me. It's been a long time since I've been in the company of such a *modest* young lady.' His gaze flickered disparagingly down towards my miniskirt.

More than ever, I wanted to plunge one of my thumbs into his eyes. But I was getting the impression that there was a chance he might actually leave me alone for a minute. And that was too tempting to resist. So I just stood there, trying to summon up a blush.

'I suppose,' he said with a sigh, 'that I can spare you five minutes.' He strolled back towards the elevator. 'Just remember, Miss Simon, that I *will* get you into that bathing suit one way or another. You see, of course, what poor Tad chose.' He nodded towards the couch. 'It would be simpler – and less painful for you in the long run – if you'd put it on yourself and spare me the trouble.'

He pulled the elevator door shut behind him.

There really *was* something wrong with him, I decided. I mean, he'd just given up a chance to see a babe like me in the buff. The guy clearly had a nacho platter where his brains should have been.

Well, that's what I told myself anyway.

Alone in Mr Beaumont's office – except for Tad and the fish, neither of whom were particularly communicative at the moment – I immediately began trying to figure out a way to escape. The windows, I knew, were hopeless. But there was a phone on Mr Beaumont's desk. I picked it up and began dialling.

'Miss Simon.' Marcus's voice, coming through the receiver, sounded amused. 'It's a house phone. You don't imagine we'd let Tad's father make any outgoing calls in his condition, do you? Please hurry up and change. We haven't much time.'

He hung up. So did I.

Half a minute wasted.

The door to the elevator was locked. So was the door on the opposite side of the room. I tried kicking it, but it was made of some kind of really thick, solid wood, and didn't budge.

I decided to turn my attention to the windows. Wrapping the end of one of the velvet curtains around my fist, I punched out a few panes of glass, then tried slamming my foot against the wooden shutters.

No good. They appeared to have been nailed permanently shut.

Three minutes left.

I looked around for a weapon. My plan, I decided, since escape appeared to be impossible, was to climb the bookshelf behind the back of the elevator door. When Marcus came though that door, I'd leap down upon him, and point a sharp object at his throat. Then I'd use him as a hostage to make my way past the two thugs.

OK, so it was a little *Xena, Warrior Princess*. Hey, it was a plan, all right? I never said it was a good one. It was just the best one I could come up with under the circumstances. I mean, it wasn't as if anybody was going to come bursting in to rescue me. I didn't see how anybody could – except for maybe Jesse, who was pretty slick at walking through walls and stuff.

Only Jesse didn't know I needed him. He didn't know I was in trouble. He didn't even know where I was.

And I had no way of letting him know either.

A shard of glass, I decided, would make an excellent, very threatening weapon, and so I looked for a particularly lethal-looking one amid the rubble I'd made of a few of Mr Beaumont's windows.

Two minutes.

Holding my shard of glass in my hand – wishing I had my ghost-busting gloves with me so I'd be sure not to cut myself – I scrambled up the bookshelf, no easy feat in three-inch heels.

One and half minutes.

I glanced over at Tad. He lay limp as a rag doll, his bare chest rising and falling in a gentle, rhythmic motion. It was quite a nice-looking chest actually. Not as nice looking, maybe, as Jesse's. But still, in spite of his uncle being a murderer, and his dad being foreman at the cracker factory – not to mention the whole basketball thing – I wouldn't

166

have minded resting my head against it. His chest, I mean. You know, under other circumstances, Tad actually being conscious being one of them.

But I'd never have the chance if I didn't get us out of this alive.

There was no sound in the room, save Tad's steady breathing and the burbling of the aquarium.

The aquarium.

I looked at the aquarium. It made up most of one whole wall of the office. How, I wondered, did those fish get fed? The tank was built into the wall. I could detect no convenient trapdoor through which someone might sprinkle food. The tank had to be accessed through the room next door.

The room I couldn't get to because the door to it was locked.

Unless.

Thirty seconds.

I dropped down from the bookshelf and began striding towards the aquarium.

I could hear the elevator begin to hum. Marcus, right on time, was on his way back. Needless to say, I had not put on my swimsuit like a good little girl. Although I did grab it – along with the wheeled swivel chair that had been behind Mr Beaumont's desk – as I walked towards the fish tank.

The humming of the elevator stopped. I heard the doorknob turn. I kept walking. The chairs' wheels were noisy on the parquet floor.

The door to the elevator opened. Marcus, seeing that I had not done as he asked, shook his head.

'Miss Simon,' he said, in a disappointed tone. 'Are we being difficult?'

I positioned the swivel chair in front of the aquarium.

Then I lifted a foot and balanced it on top of the seat. From one finger, I dangled the bathing suit.

'Sorry,' I said apologetically. 'But dead's never been my colour.'

Then I grabbed that chair, and flung it with all my might at the glass of that giant fish tank.

Twenty

The next thing I knew there was a tremendous crash. Then a wall of water, glass and exotic marine life was coming at me.

It knocked me flat on to my back. A tidal wave hit me with the weight of a freight train, pushing me to the floor, then flattening me against the far wall of the room. The wind knocked out of me, I lay there a second, soaked, coughing up briny water, some of which I accidentally swallowed.

When I opened my eyes, all I could see were fish. Big fish, little fish, trying to swim through the three inches of water that lay upon the wood floor, opening and closing their mouths in a pathetic attempt to snatch a few more seconds of life. One fish in particular had washed up next to me, and it stared at me with eyes almost as glassy and lifeless as Marcus's had been when he'd been explaining how he intended to kill me.

Then a very familiar voice cut through my dazed musings on the paradoxes of life and death.

'Susannah?'

I lifted my head, and was extremely surprised to see Jesse standing over me, a very worried look on his face.

'Oh,' I said. 'Hi. How did you get here?'

'You called me,' Jesse said.

How could I ever have thought, I wondered as I lay there gazing up at him, that any guy, even Tad, could ever be quite as hot as Jesse? Everything, from the tiny scar in his eyebrow, to the way his dark hair curled against the back of his neck, was perfect, as if Jesse were the original mould for the archetypal hottie.

He was polite too. Old-world manners were the only ones he knew. He leaned down and offered me his hand . . . his lean, brown, completely poison-oak-free hand.

I reached up. He helped me to my feet.

'Are you all right?' he asked, probably because I wasn't mouthing off as much as usual.

'I'm fine,' I said. Drenched and smelling of fish, but fine. 'But I didn't call you.'

From the opposite corner of the room came a very low snarl.

Marcus was struggling to get to his feet, but he kept slipping on all the water and fish. 'What the *hell* did you do that for?' he wanted to know.

I couldn't actually remember. I think maybe when the water hit me, I'd banged my head against something. Wow, I thought. Amnesia. Cool. I'd get out of tomorrow's Geometry quiz for sure.

Then my gaze fell on Tad – still sleeping peacefully on the couch, an exotic-looking fish flopping in death throes on his bare legs – and I remembered.

Oh, yeah. Tad's uncle Marcus was trying to kill us. *Would* kill us, too, if I didn't stop him.

I'm not sure I was really thinking straight. All I could remember from before the water hit was that it had been important, for some reason, for me to get on to the other side of that fish tank.

And so I waded through all that water – thinking to

170

myself, My boots are *so* ruined – and climbed up on to what was now just a raised platform, like a stage, looking out across a sea of slapping fishtails. The accent lights, still buried in the coloured gravel at the bottom of the tank, shined up on me.

'Susannah,' I heard Jesse say. He'd followed me, and now stood looking up at me curiously. 'What are you doing?'

I ignored him – and Marcus, too, who was still swearing as he tried to get across the room without getting his Cole-Haans more wet than they already were.

I stood inside the ruined aquarium and looked up. As I'd suspected, the fish were fed from a room behind the tank . . . a room in which there was nothing except aquarium maintenance equipment. The locked door from Mr Beaumont's office led into this room. There was no other form of egress.

Not that it mattered now, of course.

'Get down from there.' Marcus sounded really mad. 'Get down there from there, by God, or I'll climb in and fish you out—'

Fish me out. That struck me as kind of amusing under the circumstances. I started to laugh.

'Susannah,' Jesse said. 'I think—'

'We'll see how hard you're laughing,' Marcus bellowed, 'when I get through with you, you stupid bitch.'

I stopped laughing all of a sudden.

'Susannah,' Jesse said. Now he *really* sounded worried.

'Don't worry, Jesse,' I said, in a perfectly calm voice. 'I've got this one under control.'

'*Jesse?*' Marcus looked around. Not seeing anyone else in the room, however, but Tad, he said, 'It's Marcus. I'm Marcus, remember? Now, come on down here. We don't have any more time for these childish games . . .'

I bent down and seized one of the accent lights that

171

glowed, hidden in the sand at the bottom of the tank. Shaped like a small floodlight, it proved to be very hot in my hands when I touched it.

Marcus, realizing I wasn't going to come with him on my own accord, sighed, and reached into his suit coat, which was wet and smelly now. He'd have to change before his lunch meeting.

'OK, you want to play games?' Marcus pulled something made of shiny metal from his breast pocket. It was, I realized, a tiny little gun. A twenty-two, from the looks of it. I knew from having watched so many episodes of *Cops*.

'See this?' Marcus pointed the muzzle at me. 'I don't want to have to shoot you. The coroner tends to be suspicious of drowning victims bearing gunshot wounds. But we can always let the propellers dismember you so no one will actually be able to tell. Maybe just your head will toss up on to shore. Wouldn't your mother love *that*? Now, put the light down and let's go.'

I straightened, but I didn't put the light down. It came up with me, along with the black, rubber-coated cord that had grounded it beneath the sand.

'That's right,' Marcus said, looking pleased. 'Put the light down, and let's go.'

Jesse, standing in the water beside my would-be assassin, looked extremely interested in what was going on. 'Susannah,' he said. 'That is a gun he is holding. Do you want me to—'

'Don't worry, Jesse,' I said, approaching the edge of the tank, where there'd once been a wall of glass – before I'd broken it, that is. 'Everything's under control.'

'Who the hell is Jesse?' Marcus, I realized, was getting testy. 'There is no Jesse here. Now put the light down and let's—'

172

I did what he said. Well, sort of. That is, I wrapped the cord that was attached to the light around my left hand. Then with my other hand, I pulled the bulb so that the cord came popping right out of the back of the socket.

Then I stood there holding the lamp in one hand, and the cord with frayed wires now sticking out of one end of it in the other.

'That's great,' Marcus said. 'You broke the light. You really showed me. Now –' his voice rose – '*get down here!*'

I stepped up to the edge of the tank.

'I am not,' I informed Marcus, 'stupid.'

He gestured with the gun. 'Whatever you say. Just—'

'Nor,' I added, 'am I a bitch.'

Marcus's eyes widened. Suddenly, he realized what I was up to.

'No!' he shrieked.

But it was way too late. I had already thrown the cord into the murky water at Marcus's feet.

There was a brilliant blue flash and a lot of popping noises. Marcus screamed.

And then we were plunged into impenetrable darkness.

Twenty-one

Well, OK not really impenetrable. I could still see Jesse, glowing the way he did.

'That,' he said, looking down at the moaning Marcus, 'was very impressive, Susannah.'

'Thanks,' I said, pleased to have won his approval. It happened so rarely. I was glad I'd listened to Doc during one of his recent electrical safety lectures.

'Now, do you think you want to tell me,' Jesse asked, moving to offer me a steadying hand as I climbed down from the aquarium, 'just what is going on here? Is that your friend Tad on the couch there?'

'Uh-huh.' Before stepping down, I bent down, searching for the cord along the floor. 'Step over here, will you, so I can—' Jesse's glow, subtle as it was, soon revealed what I was looking for. 'Never mind.' I pulled the cord back up into the aquarium. 'Just in case,' I said, straightening and climbing out of the aquarium; 'they get the circuit breaker fixed before I'm out of here.'

'Who is *they*? Susannah, what is going on here?'

'It's a long story,' I said. 'And I'm not sticking around to tell it. I want to be out of here when he –' I nodded towards Marcus, who was moaning more loudly now – 'wakes up.

He's got a couple of thick-necked compadres waiting for me, too, in case—' I broke off.

Jesse looked at me questioningly. 'What is it?'

'Do you smell that?'

Stupid question. I mean, after all, the guy's dead. Can ghosts smell?

Apparently so, since he went, 'Smoke.'

A single syllable, but it sent a chill down my spine. Either that, or a fish had found it's way inside my sweater.

I glanced at the aquarium. Beyond it, I could see a rosy glow emanating from the room next door. Just as I had suspected, by giving Marcus a giant electric shock, I had managed to spark a fire in the circuit panel. It appeared to have spread to the walls around it. I could see the first tiny licks of orange leaping out from behind the wood panelling.

'Great,' I said. The elevator was useless without electricity. And as I knew only too well, there was no other way out of that room.

Jesse wasn't quite the defeatist I was however.

'The windows,' he said, and hurried towards them.

'It's no good.' I leaned against Mr Beaumont's desk and picked up the house phone. Dead, just as I'd expected. 'They're nailed shut.'

Jesse glanced at me over his shoulder. He looked amused. 'So?' he said.

'So.' I slammed the receiver down. '*Nailed*, Jesse. As in impossible to budge.'

'For you, maybe.' Even as he said it, the wooden shutters over the window closest to me began to tremble ominously as if blown by some unseen gale. 'But not for me.'

I watched, impressed. 'Golly gee, Mr,' I said. 'I forgot all about your superpowers.'

Jesse's look went from amused to confused. 'My what?'

'Oh.' I dropped the imitation I'd been doing of a kid from an episode of *Superman*.

'Never mind.'

I heard, above the sound of nails screaming as if caught in the suck zone of an F5 tornado, people shouting. I glanced towards the elevator. The thugs, apparently concerned for their employer's welfare, were calling his name up the shaft.

I guess I didn't blame them. Smoke was steadily filling the room. I could hear small eruptions now as chemicals – most likely of the hazardous nature – used in the upkeep of Mr Beaumont's fish tank burst into flames next door. If we didn't get out of there soon, I had a feeling we'd all be inhaling some pretty toxic fumes.

Fortunately, at that moment the shutters burst off first one and then another of the windows, with all the force as if a hurricane had suddenly ripped them off. Blam! And then blam again. I'd never seen anything like it before, not even on the Discovery Channel.

Grey light rushed in. It was, I realized, still raining out.

I didn't care. I don't think I'd ever been so glad to see the sky, even as darkly overcast as it was. I rushed to the window closest to me and looked out, squinting against the rain.

We were, I saw, in the upper storey of the house. Below us lay the patio . . .

And the pool.

The shouting up the elevator shaft was growing louder. The thicker the smoke grew, apparently, the more frantic the thugs became. God forbid one of them should think to dial 911. Then again, considering the career choices they'd made, that number probably didn't hold much appeal for them.

I measured the distance between myself and the deep end of the pool.

'It can't be more than twenty feet.' Jesse, observing my calculations, nodded to Marcus. 'You go, I'll look after him.' His dark-eyed gaze flicked towards the elevator shaft. 'And them, if they make any progress.'

I didn't ask what he meant by 'looking after'. I didn't have to. The dangerous light in his eyes said it all.

I glanced at Tad. Jesse followed my gaze, then rolled his eyes, the dangerous light extinguished. He muttered some stuff in Spanish.

'Well, I can't just leave him here,' I said.

'No.'

Which was how, a few seconds later, Tad, supported by me, but transported via the Jesse-kinetic connection, ended up perched on the sill of one of those windows Jesse had blown open for me.

The only way to get Tad into the pool – and to safety – was to drop him into it out the window. This was a risky enough endeavour without having an inferno blazing next door, and hired assassins bearing down on one. I had to concentrate. I didn't want to do it wrong. What if I missed and he smacked on to the patio instead? Tad could break his poison-oaky neck.

But I didn't have much choice in the matter. It was either turn him into a possible pancake, or let him be barbecued for true. I went with the possible pancake, thinking that he was likelier to heal in time for the prom from a cracked skull than third-degree burns, and, after aiming as best I could, I let go. He fell backwards, like a scuba diver off the side of a boat, tumbling once through the sky and doing what Dopey would call a pretty sick inverted spin (Dopey is an avid, if untalented, snowboarder).

Fortunately, Tad's sick inverted spin ended with him floating on his back in the deep end of his father's pool.

Of course, to guarantee he didn't drown – unconscious people aren't the best swimmers – I jumped in after him . . . but not before one last look around.

Marcus was finally starting to regain consciousness. He was coughing a little because of the smoke, and splashing around in the fishy water. Jesse stood over him, looking grim-faced.

'Go, Susannah,' he said when he noticed I'd hesitated.

I nodded. But there was still one thing I had to know.

'You're not . . .' I didn't want to, but I had to ask it. 'You're not going to kill him, are you?'

Jesse looked as incredulous as if I'd asked him if he were going to serve Marcus a slice of cheesecake. He said, 'Of course not. *Go.*'

I went.

The water was warm. It was like jumping into a giant bathtub. When I'd swum up to the surface – not exactly easy in boots, by the way – I hurried to Tad's side . . .

Only to find that the water had revived him. He was splashing around, looking confused and taking in great lungfuls of water. I smacked him on the back a couple of times, and steered him to the side of the pool, which he clung to gratefully.

'S-Sue,' he sputtered, bewilderedly. 'What are *you* doing here?' Then he noticed my leather jacket. 'And why aren't you wearing a bathing suit?'

'It's a long story,' I said.

He looked even more confused after that, but that was all right. I figured with as much stuff as he was going to have to deal with – his dad being a Prozac candidate, his uncle a serial killer – he didn't need to have all the gory details spelled out for him right away. Instead, I guided him over towards the shallow end. We'd only been standing there a minute before Mr Beaumont opened the sliding glass door and stepped outside.

'Children,' he said. He was wearing a silk dressing gown and his bedroom slippers. He looked very excited. 'What are you doing in that pool? There's a fire! Get out of the house at once.'

Even as he said it, I could hear, off in the distance, the whine of a siren. The fire department was on its way. Someone, anyway, had dialled 911.

'I warned Marcus,' Mr Beaumont said, as he held out a big fluffy towel for Tad to step into, 'about the wiring in my office. I had a feeling it was faulty. My telephone absolutely would not make outgoing calls.'

Still standing in the waist-high water, I followed Mr Beaumont's gaze, and found myself looking up at the window I'd just leaped from. Smoke was billowing out of it. The fire seemed to be contained in that section of the house, but still, it looked pretty bad. I wondered if Marcus and his thugs had gotten out in time.

And then someone stepped up to the window and looked down at me.

It wasn't Marcus. And it wasn't Jesse either, though this person was giving off a tell-tale glow.

It was someone who waved cheerfully down at me.

Mrs Deirdre Fiske.

Twenty-two

I never saw Marcus Beaumont again.

Oh, stop worrying: he didn't croak. Of course, the firemen looked for him. I told them I thought there was at least one person trapped in that burning room, and they did their best to get in there in time to save him.

But they didn't find anyone. And no human remains were discovered by the investigators who went in after the fire was finally put out. They found an awful lot of burned fish, but no Marcus Beaumont.

Marcus Beaumont was officially missing.

Much in the same way, I realized, that his victims had gone missing. He simply vanished, as if into thin air.

A lot of people were puzzled by the disappearance of this prominent businessman. In later weeks, there would be articles about it in the local papers, and even a mention on one cable news network. Interestingly, the person who knew the most about Marcus Beaumont's last moments before he vanished was never interviewed, much less questioned, about what might have led up to his bizarre disappearance.

Which is probably just as well, considering the fact that she had way more important things to worry about. For instance, being grounded.

That's right. Grounded.

If you think about it, the only thing I'd really done wrong on the day in question was dress a little less conservatively than I should have. Seriously. If I'd gone Banana Republic instead of Betsey Johnson, none of this might have happened. Because then I wouldn't have been sent home to change, and Marcus would never have gotten his mitts on me.

On the other hand, then he'd still probably be going around, slipping environmentalists into cement booties and tossing them off the side of his brother's yacht . . . or however it was he got rid of all those people without ever being caught. I never really did get the full story on that one.

In any case, I got grounded, completely unjustly, although I wasn't exactly in a position to defend myself . . . not without telling the truth, and I couldn't, of course, do that.

I guess you could imagine how it must have looked to my mother and stepfather when the cop car pulled up in front of our house and Officer Green opened the back door to reveal . . . well, me.

I looked like something out of a movie about post-apocalyptic America. *Tank Girl*, but without the awful haircut. Sister Ernestine wasn't going to have to worry about me showing up to school in Betsey Johnson ever again either. The skirt was completely ruined, as was my cashmere sweater set. My fabulous leather motorcycle jacket might be all right, someday, if I can ever figure out a way to get the fishy smell out of it. The boots, however, are a lost cause.

Boy, was my mom mad. And not because of my clothes either.

Interestingly, Andy was even madder. Interestingly because, of course, he's not even my real parent.

But you should have seen the way he lit into me right there in the living room. Because of course I'd had to explain to

181

them what it was I'd been doing at the Beaumonts' place when the fire broke out, instead of being where I was supposed to have been: school.

And the only lie I could think of that seemed the least bit believable was my newspaper article story.

So I told them that I'd skipped school in order to do some follow-up work on my interview with Mr Beaumont.

They didn't believe me of course. It turned out they knew I'd been sent home from school to change clothes. Father Dominic, alarmed when I didn't return in a timely fashion, had immediately called my mother and stepfather at their respective places of work to alert them to the fact that I was missing.

'Well,' I explained. 'I was on my way home to change when Mr Beaumont's brother drove by and offered me a ride, and so I took it, and then when I was sitting in Mr B's office, I started to smell smoke, and so I jumped out the window . . .'

OK, even I have to admit that the whole thing sounded super suspicious. But it was better than the truth, right? I mean, were they really going to believe that Tad's uncle Marcus had been trying to kill me because I knew too much about a bunch of murders he'd committed for the sake of urban sprawl?

Not very likely. Even Tad didn't try that one on the cops who showed up along with the fire department, and demanded an explanation as to why he was hanging around the house in a swimsuit on a school-day. I guess he didn't want to get his uncle in trouble since it would look bad for his dad and all. He started lying like crazy about how he had a cold, and the doctor had recommended he try to clear his sinuses by sitting for long bouts in his hot tub (good one: I was definitely going to have to remember it for future reference – Andy was talking about building a hot tub on to our deck out back).

Tad's father, God bless him, denied both our stories completely, insisting he'd been in his room waiting for his lunch to be delivered when one of the servants had informed him that his office was in flames. No one had said anything about Tad having stayed home with a cold, or a girl waiting for an interview with him.

Fortunately, however, he also claimed that while waiting for his lunch to be delivered, he'd been taking a nap in his coffin.

That's right: his *coffin*.

This caused a number of raised eyebrows, and eventually, it was decided that Mr Beaumont ought to be admitted to the local hospital's psychiatric floor for a few days' observation. This, as you might understand, necessarily cut off any conversation Tad and I might have had at the time, and while he went off with EMS and his father, I was unceremoniously led to a squad car and, eventually, when the cops remembered me, driven home.

Where, instead of being welcomed into the bosom of my family, I received the bawling out of a lifetime.

I'm not even kidding. Andy was enraged. He said I should have gone straight home, changed clothes, and gone straight back to school. I had no business accepting rides from anyone, particularly wealthy businessmen I hardly knew.

Furthermore, I had skipped school, and no matter how many times I pointed out that a) I'd actually been kicked *out* of school, and b) I'd been doing an assignment *for* school (at least according to the story I told him), I had, essentially, betrayed everyone's trust. I was grounded for one week.

I tell you, it was almost enough to make me consider telling the truth.

Almost. But not quite.

I was getting ready to slink upstairs to my room – in order to 'think about what I'd done' – when Dopey strolled in and casually announced that, by the way, on top of all my other sins, I had also punched him very hard in the stomach that morning for no apparent reason.

This, of course, was an outright lie, and I was quick to remind him of this: I had been provoked, unnecessarily so. But Andy, who does not condone violence for any reason, promptly grounded me for another week. Since he also grounded Dopey for whatever it was he had said that had led to my punching him, I didn't mind too much, but still, it seemed a bit extreme. So extreme, in fact, that after Andy had left the room, I sort of had to sit down, exhausted in the wake of his rage, which I had never before seen unleashed – well, not in *my* direction anyway.

'You really,' my mother said, taking a seat opposite me, and looking a bit worriedly down at the slip cover on which I was slumped, 'should have let us know where you were. Poor Father Dominic was frightened out of his mind for you.'

'Sorry,' I said woefully, fingering the remnants of my skirt. 'I'll remember next time.'

'Still,' my mother said. 'Officer Green told us that you were very helpful during the fire. So I guess . . .'

I looked at her. 'You guess what?'

'Well,' my mother said. 'Andy doesn't want me to tell you now, but . . .'

She actually got up – my mother, who had once interviewed Yasser Arafat – and slunk out of the room, ostensibly to check whether or not Andy was within earshot.

I rolled my eyes. Love. It could make a pretty big sap out of you.

As I rolled my eyes, I noticed that my mother, who always gets a lot of nervous energy in a crisis, had spent the time that I'd been missing hanging up more pictures in the living room. There were some new ones, ones I hadn't seen before. I got up to inspect them more closely.

There was one of her and my dad on their wedding day. They were coming down the steps of the courthouse where they'd been married, and their friends were throwing rice at them. They looked impossibly young and happy. I was surprised to see a picture of my mom and dad right alongside the pictures of my mom's wedding to Andy.

But then I noticed that beside the photo of my mom and dad was a picture from what had to have been Andy's wedding to his first wife. This was more of a studio portrait than a candid shot. Andy was standing, looking stiff and a little embarrassed, next to a very skinny, hippyish-looking girl with long, straight hair.

A hippyish-looking girl who seemed a little familiar.

'Of course she does,' a voice at my shoulder said.

'Jees, Dad,' I hissed, whirling around. 'When are you going to stop doing that?'

'You are in a heap of trouble, young lady,' my father said. He looked sore. Well, as sore as a guy in jogging pants could look. 'Just what were you thinking?'

I whispered, 'I was thinking of making it safe for people to protest the corporate destruction of northern California's natural resources without having to worry about being sealed up in an oil drum and buried ten feet under.'

'Don't get smart with me, Susannah. You know what I'm talking about. You could have been killed.'

'You sound like *him*.' I rolled my eyes towards Andy's picture.

'He did the right thing, grounding you,' my father said,

185

severely. 'He's trying to teach you a lesson. You behaved in a thoughtless and reckless manner. And you shouldn't have hit that kid of his.'

'Dopey? Are you *joking*?'

But I could tell he was serious. I could also tell that this was one argument I wasn't going to win.

So instead, I looked at the picture of Andy and his first wife, and said sullenly, 'You could have told me about her, you know. It would have made my life a whole lot simpler.'

'I didn't know either,' my dad said with a shrug. 'Not until I saw your mom hang up the photo this afternoon.'

'What do you mean, you didn't know?' I glared at him. 'What was with all the cryptic warnings, then?'

'Well, I knew Beaumont wasn't the Red you were looking for. I told you that.'

'Oh, big help,' I said.

'Look.' My dad seemed annoyed. 'I'm not all-knowing. Just dead.'

I heard my mother's footsteps on the wood floor. 'Mom's coming,' I said. 'Scat.'

And Dad, for once, did as I asked, so that when my mother returned to the living room, I was standing in front of the wall of photos, looking very demure – well, for a girl who'd practically been burned alive anyway.

'Listen,' my mother whispered.

I looked away from the picture. My mother was holding an envelope. It was a bright pink envelope, covered with little hand-drawn hearts and rainbows. The kind of hearts and rainbows Gina always put on her letters to me from back home.

'Andy wanted me to wait to tell you about this,' my mom said in a low voice, 'until after your grounding was up. But I can't. I want you to know I've spoken with Gina's mom, and she's agreed to let us fly Gina out here for a visit during her school's Spring Break next month—'

My mother broke off as I flung both my arms around her neck.

'Thank you!' I cried.

'Oh, honey,' my mom said, hugging me – although a little tentatively, I noticed, since I still smelt like a fish. 'You're welcome. I know how much you miss her. And I know how tough it's been on you, adjusting to a whole new high school, and a whole new set of friends – and to having stepbrothers. We're so proud of how well you're doing.' She pulled away from me. I could tell she'd wanted to go on hugging me, but I was just too gross even for my own mother. 'Well, up until now, anyway.'

I looked down at Gina's letter, which my mom had handed to me. Gina was a terrific letter writer. I couldn't wait to go upstairs and read it. Only . . . only something was still bothering me.

I looked back over my shoulder at the photo of Andy and his first wife.

'You hung up some new pictures, I see,' I said.

My mom followed my gaze. 'Oh, yes. Well, it kept my mind occupied while we were waiting to hear from you. Why don't you go upstairs and get yourself cleaned up? Andy's making individual pizzas for dinner.'

'His first wife,' I said, my eyes still glued to the photo. 'Dopey's – I mean, Brad's – mom. She died, right?'

'Uh-huh,' my mother said. 'Several years ago.'

'What of?'

'Ovarian cancer. Honey, be careful where you put those clothes when you take them off. They're covered with soot. Look, there's black gunk now all over my new Pottery Barn slip covers.'

I stared at the photo.

'Did she . . .' I struggled to formulate the correct question. 'Did she go into a coma or something?'

My mother looked up from the slip cover she'd been yanking from the armchair where I'd been lounging.

'I think so,' she said. 'Yes, towards the end. Why?'

'Did Andy have to . . .' I turned Gina's letter over and over in my hands. 'Did they have to pull the plug?'

'Yes.' My mother had forgotten about the slip cover. Now she was staring at me, obviously concerned. 'Yes, as a matter of fact, they had to ask that she be taken off life support at a certain point since Andy believed she wouldn't have wanted to live like that. Why?'

'I don't know.' I looked down at the hearts and rainbows on Gina's envelope. *Red.* I had been so stupid. *You know me,* Doc's mother had insisted. God, I should so have my mediator licence revoked. If there were a licence, which, of course, there isn't.

'What was her name?' I asked, nodding my head towards the photo. 'Brad's mom, I mean?'

'Cynthia,' my mother said.

Cynthia. God, what a loser I am.

'Honey, come help me, would you?' My mother was still futzing with the chair I'd been sitting in. 'I can't get this one cushion loose—'

I tucked Gina's envelope into my pocket and went to help my mother. 'Where's Doc?' I asked. 'I mean, David.'

My mother looked at me curiously. 'Upstairs in his room, I think, doing his homework. Why?'

'Oh, I just have to tell him something.'

Something I should have told him a long time ago.

Twenty-three

'So?' Jesse asked. 'How did he take it?'

'I don't want to talk about it.'

I was stretched out on my bed, totally without make-up, attired in my oldest jogging clothes. I had a new plan: I had decided I was going to treat Jesse exactly the way I would my stepbrothers. That way, I'd be guaranteed not to fall in love with him.

I was flipping through a copy of *Vogue* instead of doing my Geometry homework like I was supposed to. Jesse was on the window seat – of course – petting Spike.

Jesse shook his head. 'Come on,' he said. It always sounded strange to me when Jesse said things like *Come on*. It seemed so strange coming out of a guy who was wearing a shirt with laces instead of buttons. 'Tell me what he said.'

I flipped a page of my magazine. 'Tell me what you guys did to Marcus.'

Jesse looked a little too surprised by the question. 'We did nothing to him.'

'Baloney. Where'd he go then?'

Jesse shrugged and scratched Spike beneath the chin. The stupid cat was purring so loud, I could hear it all the way across the room.

'I think he decided to travel for a while.' Jesse's tone was deceptively innocent.

'Without any money? Without his credit cards?' One of the things the firemen had found in the room was Marcus's wallet . . . and his gun.

'There is something to be said –' Jesse gave Spike a playful swat on the back of the head when the cat took a lazy swipe at him – 'for seeing this great country of ours on foot. Maybe he will come to have a better appreciation for its natural beauty.'

I snorted, and turned a page of my magazine. 'He'll be back in a week.'

'I think not.'

He said it with such certainty that I instantly became suspicious.

'Why not?'

Jesse hesitated. He didn't want to tell me, I could tell.

'What?' I said. 'Telling me, a mere living being, is going to violate some spectral code?'

'No,' Jesse said with a smile. 'He's not coming back, Susannah, because the souls of the people he killed won't let him.'

I raised my eyebrows. 'What do you mean?'

'In my day, it was called bedevilment. I don't know what they call it now. But your intervention had a rallying effect on Mrs Fiske and the three others whose lives Marcus Beaumont took. They have banded together, and will not rest until he has been sufficiently punished for his crimes. He can run from one end of the earth to the other, but he will never escape them. Not until he dies himself. And when that happens –' Jesse's voice was hard – 'he will be a broken man.'

I didn't say anything. I couldn't. As a mediator, I knew I

shouldn't approve of this sort of behaviour. I mean, ghosts should not be allowed to take the law into their own hands any more than the living should.

But I had no particular fondness for Marcus, and no way of proving that he'd killed those people anyway. He'd never be punished, I knew, by inhabitants of this world. So was it so wrong that he be punished by those who lived in the next?

I glanced at Jesse out of the corner of my eyes, remembering that, from what I'd read, no one had ever been convicted of *his* murder either.

'So,' I said. 'I guess you did the same thing, huh, to the, um, people who killed you, right?'

Jesse didn't fall for this sly question though. He only smiled, and said, 'Tell me what happened with your brother.'

'Stepbrother,' I reminded him.

And I wasn't going to tell Jesse about my interview with Doc, any more than Jesse was going to tell me diddly about how he'd died. Only in my case, it was because what had happened with Doc was just too excruciatingly embarrassing to go into. Jesse didn't want to talk about how he'd died because . . . well, I don't know. But I doubt it's because he's embarrassed about it.

I had found Doc exactly where my mother had told me he'd be, in his room doing his homework, a paper that wasn't due until the following month. But that was Doc for you: why put off until tomorrow homework you could be doing today?

His 'Come in', when I'd tapped at the door had been casual. He hadn't suspected it would be me. I never ventured into my stepbrothers' rooms if I could avoid it. The odour of dirty socks was simply too overwhelming.

Only since I wasn't smelling too daisy-fresh myself at that particular moment, I thought I could bear it.

He was shocked to see me, his face turning almost as red as his hair. He jumped up and tried to hide his pile of dirty underwear beneath the comforter of his unmade bed. I told him to relax. And then I sat down on that unmade bed, and said I had something to tell him.

How did he take it? Well, for one thing, he didn't ask me a lot of stupid questions like *How do you know?* He knew how I knew. He knew a little about the mediation thing. Not a lot, but enough to know that I communicate, on a somewhat regular basis, with the undead.

I guess it was the fact that it was his own mother I'd been communicating with this time that brought tears to his blue eyes . . . which freaked me out a bit. I had never seen Doc cry before.

'Hey,' I said, alarmed. 'Hey, it's OK—'

'What—' Doc was choking back a sob. I could totally tell. 'What did she l-look like?'

'What did she *look* like?' I echoed, not sure I'd heard him right. At his vigorous nod, however, I said carefully, 'Well, she looked . . . she looked very pretty.'

Doc's tear-filled eyes widened. 'She did?'

'Uh-huh,' I said. 'That's how I recognized her, you know. From the wedding photo of her and your dad, downstairs. She looked like that. Only her hair was shorter.'

Doc said, the effort he was making not to cry causing his voice to shake, 'I wish I could . . . I wish I could see her looking like that. The last time I saw her, she looked terrible. Not like in that picture. You wouldn't have recognized her. She was in a c-coma. Her eyes were sunken in. And there were all these tubes coming out of her—'

Even though I was sitting like a foot away from him, I felt the shudder that ran through him. I said gently, 'David, what you did, when you guys made the decision to let her go . . .

192

it was the right thing. It was what she wanted. That's what she needs to make sure you understand. You know it was the right thing, don't you?'

His eyes were so deeply pooled in tears, I could hardly see his irises any more. As I watched, one drop escaped, and trickled down his cheek, followed quickly by another on the opposite side of his face.

'I-intellectually,' he said. 'I guess. B-but—'

'It was the right thing,' I repeated firmly. 'You've got to believe that. She does. So stop beating yourself up. She loves you very much—'

That did it. Now the tears were coming down in full force.

'She said that?' he asked in a broken voice that reminded me that he was, after all, still a pretty young kid, and not the superhuman computer he sometimes acts like.

'Of course she did.'

She hadn't, of course, but I'm sure she would have if she hadn't been so disgusted by my gross incompetency.

Then Doc did something that completely shocked me: he flung both his arms around my neck.

This kind of impassioned display was so unlike Doc, I didn't know what to do. I sat there for one awkward moment, not moving, afraid that if I did, I might gouge his face with some of the rivets on my jacket. Finally, however, when he didn't let go, I reached up and patted him uncertainly on the shoulder.

'It's OK,' I said lamely. 'Everything is going to be OK.'

He cried for about two minutes. His clinging to me, crying like that, gave me a strange feeling. It was kind of a protective feeling.

Then he finally leaned back and, embarrassed, wiped his eyes again and said, 'Sorry.'

I said, 'It's no big deal,' even though of course it was.

193

'Suze,' he said. 'Can I ask you something?'

Expecting more questions about his mother, I said, 'Sure.'

'Why do you smell like fish?'

I went back to my room a little while later, shaken not just by Doc's emotional reaction to the message I'd delivered but also by something else as well. Something I had not told Doc, and which I had no intention of mentioning to Jesse either.

And that was that while I'd been hugging Doc, his mother had materialized on the opposite side of the bed, and looked down at me.

'Thank you,' she said. She was, I saw, crying about as hard as her kid. Only her tears, I was uncomfortably aware, were of gratitude and love.

With all these people crying around me, was it really any wonder that *my* eyes filled up too? I mean, come on. I'm only human.

But I really hate it when I cry. I'd much rather bleed or throw up or something. Crying is just . . .

Well, it's the worst.

You can see why I couldn't tell any of this stuff to Jesse. It was just too . . . personal. It was between Doc and his mom and me, and wild horses – or excessively cute ghosts who happened to live in my bedroom – weren't going to get it out of me.

Jesse, I saw when I glanced up from the article I'd been staring at unseeingly – *How to Tell If He Secretly Loves You*. Yeah, right. A problem I so don't have – was grinning at me.

'Still,' he said. 'You must be feeling good. It's not every mediator who single-handedly stops a murderer.'

I grunted and flipped over another page. 'It's an honour I could definitely have lived without,' I said. 'And I didn't do it single-handedly. You helped.' Then I remembered that, really, I'd had the situation well in hand by the time Jesse had shown up. So I added, 'Well, sort of.'

But that sounded ungracious. So I said grudgingly, 'Thanks for showing up the way you did.'

'How could I not? You called me.' He had found a piece of string somewhere, and now he dragged it in front of Spike, who eyed it with an expression on his face that seemed to say, 'Whadduya think, I'm stupid?'

'Um,' I said. 'I did not call you, all right? I don't know where you're getting this.'

He looked at me, his eyes darker than ever in the rays of the setting sun, which poured unmercifully into my room every night at sundown. 'I distinctly heard you, Susannah.'

I frowned. This was all getting a little too weird for me. First Mrs Fiske had shown up when all I'd been doing was thinking about her. And then Jesse did the same thing. Only I hadn't, to my knowledge, *called* either of them. I'd been *thinking* about them, true.

Jees. There was way more stuff to this mediating thing than I'd ever even suspected.

'Well, while we're on the subject,' I said, 'how come you didn't just tell me that Red was Doc's mom's nickname for him?'

Jesse threw me a perplexed look. 'How would I have known?'

True. I hadn't thought of that. Andy and my mother had bought the house – Jesse's house – only last summer. Jesse couldn't have known who Cynthia was. And yet . . .

Well, he'd known *something* about her.

Ghosts. Would I *ever* figure them out?

'What did the priest say?' Jesse asked me, in an obvious attempt to change the subject. 'When you told him about the Beaumonts, I mean?'

'Not a whole lot. He's pretty peeved at me for not having filled him in right away about Marcus and stuff.' I was careful not to add that Father D was also still ballistic over the whole Jesse issue. That, he'd promised me, was a topic we were going to discuss at length tomorrow morning at school. I could hardly wait. It was no wonder I wasn't doing so hot in Geometry if you took into account all the time I was spending in the principal's office.

The phone rang. I snatched up the receiver, grateful for an excuse not to have to go on lying to Jesse.

'Hello?'

Jesse gave me a sour look. The telephone is one modern convenience Jesse insists he could live very happily without. TV is another. He doesn't seem to mind Madonna though.

'Sue?'

I blinked. It was Tad.

'Oh, hi,' I said.

'Um,' Tad said. 'It's me. Tad.'

Don't ask me how this guy, and the guy who'd gotten away with so many murders, could be from the same gene pool. I really don't get it.

I rolled my eyes, and, throwing the copy of *Vogue* on to the floor, picked up Gina's letter and re-read it.

'I know it's you, Tad,' I said. 'How's your dad?'

'Um,' Tad said. 'Much better, actually. It looks as if someone was giving him something – something my dad seems to have thought was medicine – that may actually have been having some kind of hallucinatory effect on him. Turns out the doctors think that might be what's making him think he's . . . well, what he thinks he is.'

'Really?'

Dude, Gina wrote, in her big, loopy cursive. *Looks like I'm headin' out West to see you! Your mom rocks! So does that new stepdad*

196

of yours. *Can't wait to meet the new bros. They can't possibly be as bad as you say.*

Wanna bet?

'Yeah. So they're going to try to, you know, detox him for a while, and the hope is that once this stuff, whatever it is, is out of his system, he'll be back to his old self again.'

'Wow, Tad,' I said. 'That's great.'

'Yeah. It's going to take a while, though, since I guess he's been taking this stuff since right after my mom died. I think . . . well, I didn't tell anyone, but I'm wondering if my uncle Marcus might have been giving this stuff to my dad. Not to hurt him or anything—'

Yeah, right. He hadn't been trying to hurt him. He'd been trying to gain control of Beaumont Industries, that's all.

And he'd succeeded.

'I think he really must have thought he was helping my dad. Right after my mom died, Dad was way messed up. Uncle Marcus was only trying to help him, I'm sure.'

Just like he was just trying to help you, Tad, when he pistol-whipped you and swapped your Levis for swim trunks. Tad, I realized, had some major denial going on.

'Anyway,' Tad went on. 'I just want to say, um, thanks. I mean, for not saying anything to the cops about my uncle. I mean, we probably should have, right? But it seems like he's gone now, and it would have, you know, looked kind of bad for my dad's business—'

This conversation was getting way too weird for me. I returned to the comfort of Gina's letter.

So what should I bring? I mean, to wear. I got this totally hot pair of Miu Miu slacks, marked down to twenty bucks at Filene's, but isn't it Baywatch *weather there? The slacks are a wool blend. Also, you better get us invited to some rockin' parties while I'm there because I just got new braids, and, girlfriend, let me tell you, I look GOOD. Shauna*

197

did them, and she only charged me a buck per. Of course I have to babysit her stinking brother this Saturday, but who cares? It's so worth it.

'Well, anyway, I just called to say thanks for being, you know, so cool about everything.'

Also, Gina wrote, *I think you should know, I am very seriously thinking about getting a tattoo while I'm out there. I know, I know. Mom wasn't exactly thrilled by the tongue stud. But I'm thinking there's no reason she has to see the tattoo, if I get it where I'm thinking about getting it. If you know what I mean! XXXOOO – G*

'Also, I guess I should tell you, since my uncle's gone, and my dad's . . . you know, in the hospital . . . it looks like I have to go stay with my aunt for a while up in San Francisco. So I won't be around for a few weeks. Or at least until my dad gets better.'

I was never, I realized, going to see Tad again. To him, I would eventually become just an awkward reminder of what had happened. And why would he want to hang around someone who reminds him of the painful time when his dad was running around pretending to be Count Dracula?

I found this a little sad, but I could understand it.

P.S. Check this out! I found it in a thrift shop. Remember that whacked-out psychic we went to see that one time? The one who called you – what was it again? Oh, yeah, a mediator. Conductor of souls? Well, here you are! Nice robes. I mean it. Very Cynthia Rowley.

Tucked into the envelope with Gina's letter was a battered tarot card. It appeared to have been from a beginner's set since there was an explanation printed under the illustration, which was of an old man with a long white beard holding a lantern.

The Ninth Key, the explanation went. *Ninth card in the Tarot, the Hermit guides the souls of the dead past the temptation of illusory fires by the roadside, so that they may go straight to their higher goal.*

Gina had drawn a balloon coming from the hermit's mouth, in which she'd penned the words, *Hi, I'm Suze, I'll be your spiritual guide to the afterlife. All right, which one of you lousy spooks took my lipgloss?*

'Sue?' Tad sounded concerned. 'Sue, are you still there?'

'Yeah,' I said. 'I'm here. That's really too bad, Tad. I'll miss you.'

'Yeah,' Tad said. 'Me, too. I'm really sorry you never got to see me play.'

'Yeah,' I said. 'That's a real shame.'

Tad murmured a last goodbye in his sexy, silky voice, then hung up. I did the same, careful not to look in Jesse's direction.

'So,' Jesse said without so much as an excuse-me-for-eavesdropping-on-your-private-conversation. 'You and Tad? You are no more?'

I glared at him.

'Not,' I said stiffly, 'that it's any of your business. But yes, it appears that Tad is moving to San Francisco.'

Jesse didn't even have the decency to try to hide his grin.

Instead of letting him get to me, I picked up the tarot card Gina had sent me. It's funny, but it looked like the same one Cee Cee's aunt Pru had kept turning over when we'd been at her house. Had *I* made that happen? I wondered. Had it been because of me?

But I was certainly no great shakes as a conductor of souls. I mean, look how badly I'd messed up the whole thing with Doc's mom.

On the other hand, I *had* figured it out eventually. And along the way, I'd helped stop a murderer . . .

Maybe I wasn't quite as bad at this mediating thing as I thought.

I was sitting there in the middle of my bed, trying to figure out what I should do with the card – Pin it to my door? Or would that generate too many curious questions? Tape it up inside my locker? – when somebody banged on my bedroom door.

'Come in,' I said.

The door swung open and Dopey stood there.

'Hey,' he said. 'Dinner's ready. Dad says for you to come downst— Hey.' His normally idiotic expression turned into a grin of malicious delight. 'Is that a *cat*?'

I glanced at Spike. And swallowed.

'Um,' I said. 'Yeah. But listen, Dope – I mean, Brad. Please don't tell your—'

'You,' Dopey said, 'are . . . so . . . *busted*.'